GLASS

A NOVEL

SAM SAVAGE

COFFEE HOUSE PRESS
MINNEAPOLIS :: 2011

COFFEE HOUSE PRESS books are available to the trade through our primary distributor, Consortium Book Sales & Distribution, www.cbsd.com or (800) 283-3572. For personal orders, catalogs, or other information, write to: info@coffeehousepress.org.

Coffee House Press is a nonprofit literary publishing house. Support from private foundations, corporate giving programs, government programs, and generous individuals helps make the publication of our books possible. We gratefully acknowledge their support in detail in the back of this book.

To you and our many readers around the world,
we send our thanks for your continuing support.

LIBRARY OF CONGRESS CIP INFORMATION
Savage, Sam, 1940–
Glass : a novel / by Sam Savage.
p. cm.
ISBN 978-1-56689-273-5 (alk. paper)
1. Widows—Fiction. 2. Authorship—Fiction.
3. Self-realization in women—Fiction. 4. Marriage—Fiction.
5 Psychological fiction. I. Title.
PS3619.A84G57 2011
813´.6—DC23
2011024104

1 3 5 7 9 8 6 4 2
FIRST EDITION | FIRST PRINTING
PRINTED IN CANADA

GLASS

It would be wonderful to leap over certain obstacles and be in a superior position to the one one is in. One sees that one is, in a sense, helplessly concerned with one's concerns. One has to have the thoughts one has, one can't just have the thoughts one would like to have.

—JASPER JOHNS
(in conversation with Deborah Solomon,
the *New York Times Magazine*, June 19, 1988)

*I was much too far out all my life
And not waving but drowning.*

—STEVIE SMITH

I THINK A LOT. I think too much Clarence liked to say, when I objected to some of the piffle he would come out with, especially when he had knocked back a few. I am not going to go into that now, into his drinking or his piffle, as I am not at the moment thinking about Clarence, except insofar as I have to in order to mention him at all—you cannot talk about someone without thinking about them in *that* sense. What I was actually thinking about was traveling, though not about that either in the sense of considering it as potential action—rushing to the bus station and so forth, or even looking at colorful brochures—as if I could take a trip if I wanted, though I really do want to in some sense of wanting, in some sense of trip. To want in that way is to have a desire without attaching it to any foreseeable action—desire without hope, I guess it is. I believe the word for that sort of desire is *velleity*. I am finding that I have more and more velleities these days, and one of them is the velleity to travel, a hopeless longing to just peregrinate off somewhere. But thinking about it some more it strikes me that even velleity might be too strong, suggesting as it does a feeble impulse, so terribly feeble these days. I don't as a matter of strictest fact have a desire to travel even as something hopeless and impossible, not at the present time, not when I have only just started typing again. It is more that I sometimes like to imagine the places I might go if I were to take a trip, and that is what I was doing a few moments ago, before being distracted by the thought of Clarence, which intruded without being summoned. I was sitting at the little table by the window, where I take breakfast and where the typewriter is at the moment. I am still sitting there, obviously. My posture is erect, elbows open, forearms sloping slightly downward; I am wearing a blue dress. I intend to type up all sorts of items in addition to Clarence, and among them I expect will be some that have yet to pop into my head. I say that, and it occurs to me that in the huge heap of things stacked in my head Clarence has become just an item. Before saying it—inadvertently as I have just explained—I had not thought of him in quite that way. The table is small, round, with tapered wooden legs and a Formica top. I take breakfast here because the windows face east and I can be sitting in front of them with my cup of coffee when the sun comes up. It comes shining up over the ice cream factory, the light streams in through the big windows, and I take a first small sip. Sometimes with that first sip the words "sip and shine" come into my head and shine there. Moments like these, I suppose, are what people mean when they talk of life's little pleasures. The sun comes up, the ice cream factory roars, and sometimes I imagine the roar is the sound of the rising sun, as in the Kipling poem I loved as a child, where the dawn comes up like thunder out of China across the bay. All the windows in this room face east, but the sunlight *streams* through only one of them, the center one of three, the clear one between the two obscure, as those two are mostly covered with notes and bits of tape and through them the sunlight merely seeps, apart from a few slanting shafts that penetrate the interstices, shedding bright jagged patterns on the floor. If Rudyard Kipling could see the sun come up out of the ice cream factory across the street, he would be disappointed, I am sure. There are other days when the clouds are so thick I am not certain where the sun is exactly, and on those days I have a feeling of such oppression I find it hard to see the point of going on, and when the cloudy days come one after another without a break between them, as has been happening more frequently in recent years, things reach such a pass I find myself crying over trifles. By "things" I mean mostly my thoughts. Opening the refrigerator one morning and finding there is not any milk is such a trifle, where in fact I did sit down and cry. I woke up and it was raining again. I lay in bed listening to it fall and comforted myself by thinking about how in a few minutes I was going to be curled up with my coffee in the big armchair by the window, pictured myself looking out at the rain and feeling thankful to be dry and warm. And after that to get up in the semi-dark and walk to the kitchen and discover the milk has turned and to know that I will have to drink the coffee black or go out to the store in the rain . . . naturally I sat down and just wept. In addition to the table I have an armchair and a footstool that sits in front of the armchair, and those, along with a small sofa, a bookcase, a little corner stand that holds the telephone, and two straight-back chairs that go with the table, are all the furniture in the living room, unless one counts the radio—a yellow Sony radio on the windowsill nearest the armchair. When I sit in the armchair I rest my feet on the stool, as I have been told to do because of the swelling in my ankles, though that is not why I do it—I do it because I am more comfortable that way. I sit and look across the humps of my knees at my feet, an increasingly doleful sight in recent years, with their river deltas of blue veins. I have managed to identify the Zambezi and, I think, the Magdalena, though I need to verify the latter with a better atlas. The armchair is upholstered in a brown velvety material, the footstool is brown as well but a different brown from the chair, my feet are upholstered in flesh that beneath the scaly epiderm has grown spongy lately, retaining dimples if I poke it. When I was a child I once heard my father say of my mother that she was in a brown study, and I thought, What an odd thing to say, since we could all see that she was sitting in her car in the drive-way. I have liked the expression ever since, because of the funny pictures that come with it, though I never say it out loud anymore as none of the people I talk to now would know what it means, but sitting in my brown chair I some-times think of it. "Edna is in a brown study" is how I think of it then. By "people I talk to now" I mean the people I have been talking to lately, which would be various young people behind the counter at Starbucks, the waitress at the diner, Potts, the girls at the agency, the man in the typewriter store, and a bus driver, to the best of my recollection. I have other acquaintances who would surely know what a brown study is, but I have not been talking to any of them lately, where by "not talking to them" I don't mean that we are not on speaking terms, suggesting a mutual not-talking due to animus; it is just that lately I haven't said anything in their vicinity—last summer was when I stopped saying things in their vicinity. Another expression I like is "on the point of departure," as if there were a pinnacle or peak of some sort with departure a slope on one side and staying a slope on the other. Seen in that way staying is really a kind of backsliding: sliding back into my big brown chair. There are other phrases like that, which remind me of that one—"on the verge of despair," for example. In fact there are quite a lot of those—"on the brink of madness," "at the edge of bankruptcy," "on the fringe of respectable society," and so forth. You can see just from these phrases that every walk of life has its pitfalls. I don't say that as an excuse. I have not gone to work since the second week of January. Early one morning at an hour when on any other weekday I would have been charging down the stairs to the street, afraid of missing my bus, I did not charge down the stairs. I stood on the landing for a while, and then I went back inside. I did not deliberate; there was nothing to deliberate about. "Edna was stopped cold in her tracks by a sudden blankness" was how it felt. Of course I mean mentally charging, impelled by a fear of being late, not physically running down the steps, which would be practically suicidal at my age. I did not, on the last day I was at work, intend never to return. I had not properly packed up, and I left my sheepskin earmuffs hanging on the back of a chair. I called in sick every day at first, then every few days. After a while I stopped calling, preferring to wait until they telephoned me. Now no one telephones. I did not go to work because it was too much bother. It is something of a mystery that the typewriter is once again perched on the table. I put it here quite a few weeks ago. I dragged it from the back of the closet, having removed a great many other items—clothing, books, blankets, parts of a broken chair—piling them on the bed, in order to reach it. I intended to start typing the moment I set it down, and I actually did whack the keys a few times, to check that they were working, and I saw right away that the ribbon had dried out. That was to be expected, of course, the machine having sat in my closet for years, though I was not personally expecting it, not having thought about the ribbon at all and expecting really to be able to sit down and type. I am not sure how many years, certainly ten or eleven, since I have lived in this apartment fourteen years and after the first two or three I have not typed at all. The mystery is why I all of a sudden decided to take it up again, take up typing again after so much time without it. One day I am staring out the window or quietly eating oatmeal at my table or, as I mentioned, weeping, and the next day I am typing. I will not say merrily typing or even typing away, but typing nonetheless, accurately and at a good pace, considering. When I first moved into this apartment I was still writing letters to a few people, though I was finding it increasingly difficult to think of anything to say to them beyond the usual stuff of how are you all and I am well considering, unless I happened to be recovering from flu or some such thing, and then of course I could always mention that. It became obvious after a while that I was not saying anything more than would fit on a post-card, and I started sending postcards instead, and that was when I stopped typing, postcards being the sort of thing one writes by hand, and it must have been soon after this that I put the typewriter in the closet, it having become just one more thing to trip over. Of course one *could* write postcards on a typewriter. A drawback would be that they would come out curved and have to be placed under a book until flat again, and also, because a typewriter's letters are so much smaller than handwriting, one would be able to fit more words on the card, defeating the whole purpose of writing cards in place of letters. One would end up once again inserting all sorts of irrelevant drivel just to fill up the white space, and that seems to me the actual reason people do not usually type postcards. After all, there is nothing really wrong with mailing curved postcards; certainly there is no postal rule against it, since in any case it would be flattened in the cancellation machine or whatever they call the device that prints the wavy lines across the stamps. When I said that I am now once again typing at a good pace considering, I was referring to my age: I am typing at a good pace for someone my age, with hands like mine. I am inclined to say that my fingers look like claws. My fingers do not look like claws, though they are thinner than they ever were and the knuckles are swollen. I think they are the hands of an aver-age female person of my age. My dress is fastened at the wrist by four white buttons. I collected stamps when I was a child, without enthusiasm, because the grown-ups thought I should. My father's companies received correspondence from all over the world, and he made them save all the interesting stamps for me, ones they might otherwise have taken home to their own children. I did not enjoy collecting stamps and never bothered pasting them into the big blue albums Papa bought me, but I kept the prettiest ones near my bed in a mahogany box with an old-fashioned square-rigged sailing ship carved in bas-relief on the lid, and I looked at them now and then. The ones I liked best were from countries I had never heard of, faraway parts of the British Empire, and French Equatorial Africa, a place that because of its name impressed me as infinitely desirable. I was required to take a nap every afternoon until I was ridiculously old, and instead of sleeping I sometimes took the stamps from the box and looked at them and imagined that I was traveling to the places the stamps came from and riding elephants, encountering crocodiles, and things of that nature. I actually don't remember my daydreams from that period, just that I spent a lot of time having them, so I am only guessing when I say they included crocodiles and elephants. I mean, why wouldn't they? As time passed, and my situation became increasingly intolerable, I daydreamed more often, not just at nap time, and stayed away longer. I stayed away in the dreams—I was dreaming that I was away. By "situation" I mean ordinary life, which at that time included Mama and Papa. I must have been four or five when I finally recognized that ordinary life with them had become intolerable for me. They had brought me to my first day at kindergarten, "they" in this instance being Mama and Nurse, the large German woman who took care of me while Mama was socially whirling. She had a real name, I suppose, but if I once knew it I have forgotten it now. The words "Gertrude Klemmer" hover next to a number of my earliest recollections, though perhaps that was someone in a book. Whatever her name, she was Nurse to me, and I saw a great deal more of her than of Mama or Papa. She left when I was five or six, replaced by a series of other women, none of whom stayed for very long. I am not sure she was German; she might have been Dutch. I finally did travel to Europe several times after I was grown, to Mexico, Venezuela, and to East Africa once, for a short while, but I never went to any of the countries of my favorite stamps. Traveling as a grown-up, with all the burdens and unhappiness of being grown, turned out to be not nearly as nice as I had thought it would be when I imagined it as a child.

The blank space means I stopped typing at that point—to go look for a picture of Nurse. I had been wondering if she was German or Dutch, and I thought I would have another look at her picture. That was ridiculous, of course, to think I could find out by looking at a picture whether someone is German or Dutch, but I went and looked for it anyway. I have noticed that I am having a great many thoughts lately that don't quite make sense. As happened earlier, when I complained about being distracted by the thought of Clarence, which I accused of intruding without being summoned. In fact, after reflecting on it some more, it is not clear to me how a thought could *ever* be summoned, as I seem to have suggested then. After all, I would scarcely be in a position to summon a thought, pluck it from the enormous heap of all possible thoughts, were I not already thinking it, in some sense of thinking, in some sense of already, and of course it is less a heap than a tangle, an enormous tangle of possible thoughts, like a jungle. Summoning a thought would be like summoning a stranger from a crowd in order to find out his name. Well, I suppose you could do that with gestures or by shouting or by going over to him and plucking his sleeve, as you might do if one day you were to see someone in a railroad station whose name you would like to know, perhaps because he looks like the kind of person you would want to be friends with. To make the analogy work you have to imagine that you are not able to go over next to that person, perhaps because you are crippled or horribly tired or under arrest and are handcuffed to a policeman. You see this person you want to know, perhaps someone famous who would be able to help you out of your difficulty, but you are not allowed by some mysterious force which we won't go into now to shout or wave or even move your eyes in a significant manner. The only way you are permitted to get his attention is by calling his name, and that is just the thing you don't know and were hoping to find out. Of course we have to assume also that the people you are with, the policeman or doctor or whatever, don't know his name either, or if they do they are refusing to tell you, because they think it would be harmful for you to contact that person or perhaps harmful to them, to their position in society, especially if you are being wrongly detained, or perhaps they just do it out of spite. I feel that I am not making myself clear. I am trying to make the really simple point that summoning thoughts is out of the question: they just come, and the matter seems complicated only because it is really so simple. That is often the case, I suppose, simple things being slippery because they don't possess any angles by which one can get a firm grip on them. I find it helpful to think of the mind as like a street: cars and people and whatever, dogs, leaves, just keep coming into it, turning into it or walking or blowing into it, scraps of paper and dust, for example, in addition to leaves, and there is no telling what will turn into it next, nor is there any way to peer around the corner and see what is coming and maybe divert some of it one way or the other, perhaps by standing at the intersection and waving one's arms the way a traffic policeman does; send this car that way and that one this way, where by "cars" of course I mean thoughts, and by this way and that way I mean into the mind or not. When you think about it like that, using only concrete images, it is easy to see how absurd it is to think that one can summon thoughts. They just come. There is another matter that is related to this one in a way that is not clear to me at the moment. Possibly I could make it clear were I to think about it some more, but I am really quite tired of the whole subject. I feel that I am dithering, even though when I set out I was determined to be decisive. When I set out typing, I mean. I set out to be concise and decisive, and in the next moment a hundred things broke in, intruded of their own volition, invaded really, and as I have just finished pointing out not summoned in any way. That needs to be qualified—qualifications being another thing, in addition to intrusions, that tend to get in the way: even though one cannot summon thoughts willy-nilly out of nowhere, once they have shown themselves even partially, poked up the tips of their noses, as it were, one is able to line them up to be thought about, like distributing numbers to people at a deli counter. For example, when I typed that bit about velleities I was also on the verge of saying several other things, but I made those wait in line until I could talk about velleities, and then of course the things that crowded in with that, the furniture, the spoiled milk, the stamp collection, and so forth, right up to the man in the railroad station. In my experience it is not possible to give out more than a few numbers at a time, at least not possible to give them out in one's head. When a great many things crowd in at once, I write them down on a piece of paper, or else I forget to think about them. Sometimes I tape the paper up on a window where I can see it. The photograph I was looking for is of Nurse and me in the yard at home. I thought I had put it back in the letter box, that being what I call the cardboard box where I keep all the letters I care to preserve, as well as most of my photographs. I don't *call* it that exactly, in that I don't believe I have said those words out loud together even once, unless we count the times I almost certainly did say them when we lived in England, where that is how they like to say mailbox. We were there for only three weeks, so I couldn't have said it very often even then, but just a moment ago, when I was wondering where the photograph of Nurse had got to, I am sure I was thinking something like, "it must be in the letter box." Otherwise how could I have known where it was I was about to look? Unless, of course, I had a picture of the box in my head at the time. I am certain I did not have a picture like that in my head at the time. I often have words in my head, sometimes my own words, sometimes other people's, fragments of conversations, bits and pieces of songs and poems, pointless chatter, and little announcements like "I am going to open the window" just before I open the window, but I seldom have pictures. The photo was not in the letter box. I had used it as a bookmark, I finally remembered, in *The Lord of the Rings*, which I was trying to read a few years ago—trying once again, that is, there was such talk about it after they made it into a movie, though I was just as bored as the first time, ever so many years ago—and when I put it back on the shelf I must have forgotten to retrieve the bookmark. I had obviously forgotten, since there it was sticking out of the book. I normally use string for bookmarks, not pictures. It used to irritate Clarence when I would go back and forth in this manner, saying one thing and then another, with the second thing canceling out the first in a way that might seem fickle, and drifting sideways instead of shooting relentlessly forward, though I would not call it dithering, which sounds lax and weak-kneed. He called it vacillating, but to me it is just thinking. Clarence's mind always dove straight for what he wanted, and he said that my back-and-forthing drove him nuts. But frankly there was something almost brutal about his own thinking, if one can even call it thinking. He had no inkling of the difficulty some of us have in going forward. It is fair to say that Clarence was not a thinking person. In fact he was able to do what he did and, incidentally, write the way he wrote, only because he was simply blind to alternatives, his sentences stamping across the page like little soldiers, each armed with a dangerously active little verb. And some people loved it, because the sentences carried them right along, and like the little soldiering sentences themselves his readers were not obliged ever to think about where they were going. I have always thought this about his writing; if anyone had asked me I would have said so, even though the sentences in *The Forest at Night* are not nearly as awful as they became later. I mean awful in that particular respect; in other respects they are wonderful, of course. I expect that in the future I will want to stop typing for a variety of other reasons, other than looking for a photo, and I anticipate leaving a blank spot in those places as well. I have stopped several times already, pausing surreptitiously, so to speak, but did not think of putting in blanks then, and I don't recall where those places were, in order to go back and put them in now. Needing a minute or two to think something over might be a reason, in which case I will want to keep my hands poised above the keyboard in anticipation of going on, unless of course the thinking turns into dwelling on the past or even mulling, as it so easily can, in which case I will want to rest them in my lap. I will probably stare out the window if it comes down to mulling. Leaving off typing altogether would be another reason I might want to put in a blank space—leaving it off altogether *temporarily*, I mean, in order to busy myself elsewhere, not giving up for good, though there are quite a few things I might want to do right here at the table: draw pictures, for example, or lay my head down for a rest, or eat something, an apple, for instance, that I have found there. I might after typing a while decide to stand up due to cramps, stretching my arms above my head, stamping my feet to get the tingles out. Perhaps, if it is not cold or rainy out, after a few stretches and stamps I will open a window and look down at the street while resting my elbows on the sill, or even lie down on the rug for a few hours, like a dog. I might also stop for a lot of other reasons—because I am having lunch or have gone out to the movies; or I might be sleeping or have gone off on a trip somewhere, though that last seems unlikely, as I mentioned at the outset. I considered varying the size of the blank space according to the length of time I am away—the wider the blank the longer the time—but after thinking about it some more I decided that would not be practical: I would need just reams of blank pages if I actually were to go off on a trip, even a short one around the block, being such a slow walker. And I doubt that I am going to want to mention everything I do when I am not typing. I am not going to say, I just got up to urinate, I just got up to see if the mail has come, and so forth. I suppose that merely seeing the photograph of Nurse, when I was using it as a bookmark, having not seen it for a great many years, might be what prompted me to drag the typewriter out of the closet, though that by itself does not abolish the mystery; it only pushes it back a step, to the question of why after all that time I decided to go rummaging in the letter box in the first place. Rummaging in my mind is what I am doing. I say that, and I get a picture of someone up to the neck in balled-up newspaper; a female someone, as I can tell from the hairdo. It is dark outside my windows now. Not dark entirely, since I live on a city street where there are always lights, but fairly dark, considering. I have turned on the lights in the room, the ceiling light and the standing lamp next to the armchair. The last time I mentioned something like that the sun was shining; mentioned, that is, whether it is day or night, both of which are merely symptoms of what is really going on out there, which is planetary motion, the rotation of the earth on its axis and (for us) night following day, day following night, regardless. I say that, and I see the planet Earth, the way it looks from the moon in the photographs they brought back from that dreadful place, like a spinning blue-and-white glass marble out in the middle of nowhere. At this moment it has completed approximately three and one half spins since I took up typing again. When I was in the ninth grade our science teacher told us about the Renaissance public's reaction to the idea that the earth is round and not flat, an idea that must have been quite startling at the time. It cannot be round, people said then, or the persons living on the bottom half would have fallen off. The teacher laughed when she told us about that, because those people were so silly, and we all laughed too, and I am sure we all thought, "What silly people." I joined in, of course, even though I really had no idea why the persons on the bottom had not fallen off. It still strikes me as odd that they don't. I think something is wrong with one of the streetlights, is the reason it is so dark outside.

Last November, I think it was, I got a letter from Clarence's original publisher, from a woman who works there, whose name I have now forgotten, telling me of their plans to reissue *The Forest at Night,* since next year will be its fortieth, a thing, she said, that is hard to believe, and would I like to write a short preface? Her name was Angelina Grossman. I thought for a moment that I would write back and remind her of one or two painful things, painful to me still, I planned to say, and I trusted also painful to them, the people at Webster and Davis, now that they have had time to reflect. A dismissive scrawl, in pencil probably, on one of those plain postcards they sell at the post office, not a picture postcard. And then I thought that I would not write after all, just not respond, express in that way my indifference and contempt, and I dropped the letter in the wastebasket. Then I took it out of the wastebasket and considered. And then I tore it up. In the process of going back and forth and then trying to fit all the little torn bits together, with the tape wanting to stick to the wrong pieces, I became thoroughly worked up, distraught really. It occurred to me that if I refused they might ask Lily to do it, ask her out of spite, because of the unpleasant things I said about them at the time. Of course they have to be aware that she is not in a position to write anything, they have to know this, but I imagined them making her talk into a tape recorder, taking down her version of Clarence, a one-sided and completely truncated version, and then hiring someone to dress it up in grammatical English. That, of course, is an absurd idea, and the fact that I was able to entertain it shows how worked up and addled I was. In the end I sent Grossman a postcard with a picture of a bear on it. I told her I could not (I underlined *not*) write a short preface but that I would consider writing a long introduction or even, I said, a separate book (I underlined *separate* twice), and while there would be a lot about Clarence in it, it would not be just about him but also about my life before and after, as one could not pretend to understand Clarence without that. If that is the reason the typewriter is now on the table, it took a long time to take effect. I pulled the machine from the closet in January, I think it was, after I had practically forgotten all about the letter, which, as I mentioned, arrived in November or even October, and now it is April.

I was eating lunch this afternoon, when suddenly the doorbell rang. Not strictly eating, not actively chewing, just pushing food around on the plate—lentils from a can I opened a few days ago and forgot about until I discovered them in the refrigerator when I was looking for cheese. I ate a biggish piece of cheese while heating the lentils, and then I was not hungry anymore. I say *piece* of cheese instead of *chunk*, which is what it actually was, because *chunk* possesses a jolly ring that does not fit the atmosphere that reigned while I was eating it, which was subdued and a trifle mournful, stirring lentils at the stove. It was cheddar cheese. I don't know the brand, since it came without a wrapper from the Bread of Life Center, where I sometimes get food when I have used up my stamps. I often just take cheese when I visit the center, as I don't eat processed food, which is what people normally give to food pantries, because, I suppose, that is what poor people typically eat. It feels natural to them, I imagine. I cannot recall a time in my life when it could be said that I ate with gusto. I lack vital energy, is what Clarence used to say; lack the will to live, was how he put it. On second thought, I am the one who said that and Clarence just agreed. He nodded, is what he did, sitting beside me on the bed in the yellow-papered house after I came back from Potopotawoc. If this ever becomes a book I am going to have to say something about Potopotawoc. And I ought not to have said that the doorbell rang suddenly. After all, how else *could* it ring? Unless it were outfitted with some sort of crescendoing device that would let it gradually work its way up from a tinkle. I ought to have said that I was not *expecting* the doorbell to ring, because it had not rung for a long time, months and months, I am sure, and I was startled when it finally did, and a door *buzzer* is what it strictly is, not any sort of bell. My first thought was not to answer. A long time ago, when I was still typing seriously, I was capable of doing that, and I did not answer the telephone either, and everyone remarked how resolute I was, and they were admirative too and not at all piqued even when it was their phone call I had failed to answer, despite the fact that answering machines had not been invented yet and if a person did not answer you had to call back again and again until finally they did, perhaps wasting a good part of your day. And all the while you had no idea if they were not answering because they were just awfully busy, as in my case, or were terribly ill or were so depressed they could not bear the sound of a human voice. You could not tell if they were actively shunning you personally or were simply not home, as often happened in the case of people like Clarence, who were always on the go. The phone calls were usually for Clarence anyway, and that was another reason I did not answer them. Though I am now busy again, busy with typing, I have still not got into the swing of it, into the habit of being busy and feeling busy, so I don't have the other habits that go along with it such as not responding to buzzers. I sometimes regret that the door to my apartment is not equipped with one of the little holes you can peep through and see who is out there. Of course whoever is there could always put a finger over it, but that by itself would be a clue: it would say, for example, that the person whose finger is plugging the hole intends to surprise me, perhaps going so far as to shout "surprise!" the instant I crack the door open, assuming I would crack it open for someone who has plugged the hole. I was dwelling on this thought, on what would prompt me to open or not open and whether there are times when I might become so desperate that I would open even for someone who had a finger over the peephole, on the off chance that it was an old acquaintance being playful, when the buzzer went off again. It occurred to me that it might be a delivery person with a package for me, though on reflection that seemed far-fetched as well. "It was without expectation that Edna inched the door open and discovered Potts from the flat below," was how it finally was. Of course I knew all along that it had to be either Potts or the landlord, Potts being the only other person currently living in the building, and the landlord would be coming about the rent, which I have not paid in full since I stopped going to work. It could also have been someone from the agency, I suppose, in a pinch. I am not going to discuss the agency now. My apartment is on the top floor, the uppermost of three, and Potts lives in the flat below. Nobody lives on the first floor. When I came here an insurance company had offices down there, but it closed after a few years, and then a political campaign had head-quarters there, briefly, but it has been empty ever since. Empty of people, that is; Giamatti, the landlord, stores things there. Potts has lived in this building almost as long as I have, first with her husband and then, after he died years ago of galloping cancer, alone with a great many potted plants, an assortment of monstrous bug-eyed goldfish, and a domesticated rat. Even so we have not become friends. There is a dearth on my part of fondness for Potts, even the trifling fondness of neighborly feeling. Solitudes, I have noticed, do not attract. We do each other small favors, try not to grate on each another's nerves, and avoid needling. Potts is squat and square with large brown protuberant eyes, a small mouth that she opens and closes between sentences, as if sipping, and a short neck. With her stump-like body and quick movements she emits an impression of compact solidity, like a small appliance, a sturdy toaster. She used to possess the thoroughly un-American skill of hands-free smoking, a smoldering cigarette dangling from her lower lip at every moment, even while she talked, blinking through smoke-watered eyes. It lent her a raffish slatternly charm that vanished the instant she kicked the habit. She is leaving in a few days to visit her son in California, or maybe Texas, I don't remember, Utah possibly, where he is a petroleum engineer. I had promised to look after her plants, promised it months ago, and then forgot. She has several sons, I am not sure how many, and carries on about them with relentless fervor whenever we bump into each other, on the stairs usually, or in the little grocery store at the corner, when I make an effort to pay attention, straining. I lift my earmuffs and try not to bob about or fiddle with the merchandise while she is talking, if we are in the store, or slide my hand up and down on the stair railing, if that is where we are, but I have not managed to form a clear picture of any of them. That might not be my fault—they might just be amorphous people. I have known people with such vague personalities that a hazy picture of them is the best one can hope for. Mr. Potts was like that, and he might have passed the trait on to his sons. I called the one in Texas, if it *is* Texas, a petroleum engineer, because Potts calls him that, though I have not the vaguest idea what a petroleum engineer actually is or does. When I typed those words I was in fact typing something that for me personally is practically meaningless. Which goes to show how simple it is to think nonsense, especially when one is typing, how easy it is for language to get away from us and go off on its own, as it seems to have gotten away from the young ones. We used to talk about the fete of language, but it is really just a brawl. We had Joyce and Proust and the curious Mr. Waugh to keep us straight; now it is all comic books and dragons. And I don't know what possessed me to say a pretentious thing like solitudes do not attract. I have no idea whether they attract or not. I am not sure what kind of cancer it was that carried off Mr. Potts, since I didn't visit down there while he was sick, and then he was gone, and it seemed crass to inquire about medical details at that point. I am still curious, though, as he seemed to go from hale and hearty to defunct in an amazingly short span—short for cancer, that is: a person can die of a heart attack at the drop of a handkerchief, obviously. With Potts on vacation I will be the only person currently living in this building. She was holding a cardboard carton full of "perishables" (was how she put it)—cheese and celery and such, bananas with brown spots on the skin, milk, an open box of cornflakes. I tried to take the carton from her, but she held on when I pulled at it. She clasped it to her chest and scurried into the kitchen. I waited out on the landing. I picked at the bits of paint peeling from the walls and put the pieces in the pocket of my skirt, a black skirt with small pockets on the side. The walls are painted yellow above and brown below, dating from a time when children lived in the building, probably, in order not to show handprints, and the paint is dirty even where it is not peeling. Through the open doorway I could hear Potts in the kitchen taking things out of the box and setting them on the counter, the refrigerator door opening and closing, followed by a silence in which I seemed to hear her peering into things. She came whirring back, having popped up a perfect slice, and we went downstairs together to have a look at the plants.

Potts' apartment is the same shape as mine exactly, with a bay window like mine, but it does not produce the same sensation—it is closet-like and oppressive, not luminous and airy like mine. After a few minutes I become thoroughly desperate down there, because of the crowding-in furniture (lots of upholstery and carpets and dark things with knobs) and the potted plants and breakable knickknacks everywhere. Trapped and running out of air is how it feels exactly. I don't think she ever throws anything out, except, naturally, leftovers and garbage and the like, and worn-out clothes, I imagine. Mr. Potts's personal items are still scattered about. Even the sports magazines he obsessively read are still in an untidy stack on a little three-legged table next to his upholstered rocking chair, as if he had just stepped outside for a smoke. Last year when my toilet was clogged I went down to use the bathroom. The plaid robe he wore when he descended to the street to fetch his newspaper in the morning was still hanging from a hook on the inside of the bathroom door, and I noticed one of the pockets bulging with balled-up Kleenex. I would not like to have Clarence's stuff lying all over the place. I can just imagine coming home, in the dark perhaps, with my arms full of groceries, and tripping over his shoes. I am sure I would not think, "Oh dear, there are Clarence's shoes on the floor in the middle of the room again." That is the sort of thing I might have thought at one time, when he was in fact leaving his shoes all over the place. By "at one time" I mean all the time we were together—there was just no changing him when it came to his shoes. But if after he was gone I had kept his shoes lying around the way Potts has with Arthur's things and tripped over them then, I would think instead, "Oh dear, there are Clarence's *empty* shoes." And then, of course, I would get a pang. When I moved to this place, I did not bring anything that had belonged to Clarence. I looked in every one of our books before packing, and if he had signed his name on the flyleaf, as he invariably did when he bought a new one, I left it behind. Opening a book and finding his name, you can just imagine the pang.

We stood side by side in front of the aquarium, while Potts talked about the proper way of feeding the fish—strange deviant goldfish with short egg-shaped bodies, bulging eyes, and long drooping tails. They swam diaphanously back and forth. Climbing on a stepstool and inserting her arm up to the elbow in the water she demonstrated the correct method of removing algae from the glass with a little scraper she had purchased just for that, for me to be able to do that in case the algae becomes too much for the snails to handle, while the fish darted frantically this way and that. They did not dart, actually. Their thick bodies and overdeveloped fins made impossible anything as swift as darting, or as graceful as swimming either; they jerked themselves forward, looking like bright tadpoles trailing scarves. When she had asked me if I would water the plants, weeks ago that must have been, she did not say anything about fish; I would remember had she mentioned fish. She had written out a page of instructions about the plants and another about the fish and posted them on her refrigerator with magnets. We faced the refrigerator and read them over together—she read them aloud, and I followed with my eyes, nodding, I mean, not that we read them in chorus. I could not understand a word. We walked around the apartment, Potts in front with short quick steps, a toy that had been wound up and let run, chattering about the plants, and I a few paces behind, straining to listen, bent. Being taller than Potts I couldn't help noticing a bald spot on her crown, a salmon-colored circle the size of a half dollar on the apex of her dome. She must have developed it recently or I would have noticed before. I could not stop my mind from drifting to it, wondering what it was a symptom of and whether I ought to mention it to her, in case she had not noticed yet, or not mention it, in case it was something she was doing to herself, neurotically tugging, for example. I paused to peer into the rat's cage—not a cage, really, just an ordinary aquarium with a wire lid, like the fish tank but larger—a terrarium, properly speaking, or perhaps a vivarium. It looked empty at first, until I noticed the depilated tail protruding from a white PVC tube lying on its side in the wood shavings. "Nigel's asleep," Potts said. She tapped the wire top of the cage. Nothing moved. "He had a busy night." "I am not taking care of the rat," I said. She brightened: "Oh no, dear, a friend from the Rat and Mouse Club is taking him over to *his* house. Nigel *loves* meeting new rats." The plants needing the most water she had placed in the bathtub, filling it entirely. I can spray those with the hand shower, she said, and demonstrated the correct method, spraying water on the floor. Even with so many in the tub, there were still plants on every surface, on tables, windowsills, the back of the toilet, the counters in the kitchen. As we drew abreast of each one she told me its name and an anecdote or two, about the store she had bought it from, the time she had almost killed it with too much fertilizer, and so forth, soliloquies delivered while staring fixedly at the plant in question, as if addressing it, never up at me. It was impossible to listen to her. We ended the tour in front of a titanic fern, feather-like fronds erupting in a fountain from a large pot of shiny black ceramic, the tops reaching almost to my shoulder. This was, she said, Arthur's ultimate present to her, purchased on the last day that he still felt well enough to get about, and *it*, she explained, in addition to regular watering in the usual way, would have to be misted twice a day. She brandished a plastic spray bottle. "Important, important," she said, wagging the bottle like an admonishing finger. It was her idea to carry the plant up to my place—to spare me trips up and down the stairs, was how she put it, though of course she was thinking that I am unlikely to remember to spray it twice a day unless I am tripping over it. I am not a practical person, I am sure she knows that, and I am not oriented to nature. She gave me a geranium once, many years ago, shortly after she and her husband had moved here. I set it down someplace and forgot about it until several weeks later when I was dusting in my bedroom and noticed a pot full of dirt and twigs on the dresser. Clarence and I never stayed anywhere long enough to have plants, besides cut flowers, except at the end, and at that point no one bothered. We might have not bothered by then because of the wallpaper in the last house, which was alive with flowers. The wallpaper, that is, was alive with them; it was a flower-pattern wallpaper. They were yellow roses.

Leaning into the fern, dipping our arms up to the shoulder in foliage, we grasped the curved lip of the pot, one on each side, and hoisted. It was extremely heavy, the ceramic was slippery, and we had to set it down every three or four steps on our way up the stairs and hold it in place with our knees to prevent it tumbling back down the stairway, while we panted above it. Potts is shorter than me by a head, and each time we lifted the pot the fronds rushed into her face and knocked her glasses crooked. With both hands clinging to the pot she had no choice but to leave them that way, dangling from the tip of her nose, until it was time to pause again, and twice they fell off into the thicket of fronds, forcing us to stop while she searched for them, parting the fronds and peering and squinting as if hunting insects. At the top of the stairs we turned and maneuvered the plant through the doorway, with me backing in first. I could not right off the bat think where to put it, and I did not want Potts hanging around while we talked it over, so I suggested we just plunk it on the floor by the table, tilting my head to indicate the table with the typewriter, and I said *plunk* in order to convey the impression that I did not care in the least where it went. It is still there, on the floor next to the table. My elbow brushes against it when I operate the carriage return lever, tickling, and I have to pause and rub. Several of the fronds seem to have become broken on the way up the stairs—they are hanging sharply down like the wings of a crippled bird—or else I broke them pushing past to get to my chair. I am going to have to move it someplace else. It is one thirty in the morning. It has taken me two hours to type Potts up. In the silent interstices that open periodically in the midst of the clatter of the keys (I am tempted to write "thunder of the keys"), when I pause to think before going on (or before going back in order to bury something beneath a chain of x's), I notice how quiet everything has become, where "everything" I mean the city, or at least the portion of it beneath my window, though earlier someone in the street was shouting "Martha" again and again. I want to explain about the silence: it is the silence of a roaring, a roaring that goes on all day long and for some parts of it all night as well—roaring of compressors on the roof of the ice cream factory, ocean-like roaring of traffic on the Connector, amalgamated cacophonous roaring of people and cars mingled in the street below. I am so accustomed to it that I don't even hear it most of the time, especially in the colder seasons, when I have the windows closed, as they are now. I hear it when it stops. This is not at all what I meant to do. I intended just to mention Potts, notice her parenthetically, so to speak. "Edna, in passing, dropped a few words about Potts, a neighbor" is how it was supposed to be. I thought I would use the encounter with my neighbor as an example of the sort of thing that can happen in the blank spaces. It was not a good choice; I can see that now. It thoroughly fails to convey the depth of the tedium that defines those places, that, in fact, constitutes their blankness. I made it happen too fast, for one; and for two, even though lugging the fern up the stairs was quite taxing in a physical way, it was not boring in the least. Thanks to Potts's glasses it was even comical in a feeble way. In fact and for the most part nothing happens in the blank spaces, and when a blank space goes on and on for years, so long it would take thousands of blank pages even to hint at how long and tedious it is, an hour with Potts cannot even begin to convey it, and I don't know why I keep saying *tedium*, when it is actually much worse than that.

I am at my station early this morning. The sun is not yet above the roof of the factory, but the buses are running and the street is already choked with cars, as I can tell by the noise, and the compressors are hard at work. If I were to open the windows now, I would have to wear muffs. By "station" I mean my table, of course; I could also call it my post or even my outpost. I am on guard here, finger on the trigger, meaning the keys, in a final stand against melancholy. I am tempted to say final *desperate* stand, as in Custer's Last. I have propped the photograph against my coffee mug, where I can look at it while typing—the one of Nurse and me that I was about to discuss when I became distracted by Potts, among other items. Seven spins ago that would be. I did not type anything yesterday or the day before that, those being the blank space above. Nurse is wearing a long plain dress with big puffy pockets in front (the pockets are a different color from the dress), while I am in a short dress with ruffles and no pockets that I can see. The photo is in black and white, so my dress looks white, though I remember it as pale yellow. I have a large bow in my hair, which looks black, but it might have been dark blue or maroon—the ribbon looks black, that is, my hair was auburn, and I don't recall a bow. Neither of us is smiling. We stand next to one of the tall hedges that bordered our driveway at home, some of them carved in European fashion into the shapes of animals. My father designed them, but the actual bending and clipping was done by a gardener on a tall wooden ladder, my father shouting instructions from below. The animal in the hedge beside us seems to be a bear. In fact the bear is pretty much at the center of the photo, with Nurse and me standing off to the side, so perhaps I should not have said that the photograph is of us—it is of the bear, and we are just in it. Behind the bear is the house we lived in, a big brick house on a hill—you cannot see the hill in the picture—with several very large chimneys, which you can see, that come up along the outside walls, and a cupola on the roof, which you can only see the top of. The cupola had windows on all sides. With its six or eight sides (I have forgotten how many exactly) it resembled the top portion of a lighthouse, but it was only up there for show and did not connect to any stairway or door. I recall standing on the lawn with Papa and asking him to take me up to the cupola, and I remember him saying there was no way into it. The bay windows of this apartment remind me of the cupola, of how it might have looked from inside had I ever gone there. An expensive garden with statues, several fountains, and, as I mentioned, hedges shaped like animals surrounded the house. I was very small, when one day walking in the garden with Nurse we found a dead mole. We showed it to the gardener, Nurse pointing to it with the toe of her shoe (she wore black shoes with laces, as did the maid and cook, because they were servants, I thought, since Mama never wore shoes with laces), and he picked it up and stuffed it in his pocket. For some reason that is the clearest of all my childhood memories: whenever I think of those times for very long the mole is there. An iron fence made of tall black spears guarded the perimeter of the whole of it—house, garden, coach house, and so forth. Later, when I would show people pictures, I would tell them the fence was there to keep the animals from running off. Except for kindergarten and measles I don't remember much that happened in my life until I was five, when I was attacked on the sidewalk near our house by a large brown-and-white dog. Luckily I was rescued by the postman, though my dress was nearly torn off me. And once during a storm I tried to walk from my room to my parents' room on a narrow ledge that ran around the outside of the house beneath the windows, and I slipped and fell into a box hedge, from which Mother's driver rescued me, carrying me into the house in his arms, and to this day the odor of wet foliage brings with it a pleasurable feeling, an ever-so-slight giddiness and excitement, which I think might be due to the connection with being rescued in that way, though I don't recall why I wanted to go to my parents' room or why I didn't use the door.

Papa was a handsome man. He possessed a large blond mustache and an imposing chin, and he jutted as he walked—if you were in his way you would probably want to get out of it. It was, I imagine, this imposing and jutting way of his that had put him where he was, which was on top of the heap. Mama was a lovely woman. She possessed wide-set gray eyes, an upturned nose, a sumptuous bosom, and a difficult personality. She was given to nervous spells and vapors, read *Vogue* in French, and did not much enjoy me when I was little. Papa was given to accumulation and when not supervising rolling mills and smelters enjoyed golf, shooting pheasant, the *New York Herald Tribune*, and gadgets. He occasionally, as I recall, enjoyed me on his knee, where we played horsey, starting sedately and finishing in a gallop that threw me onto the floor once, causing my head to bleed. That is, I believe, my earliest memory of Papa. He was a genuine type of sportsman, by which I mean he did not pursue his sports merely as an aspect of something else the way Clarence did, when he, Clarence, would pursue certain sports in order to be able to write about them later, going down ferocious rivers in a rubber boat, shooting large animals, and jumping out of an airplane once, for example. Being handsome, lovely, and rich they ought to have been happy, I suppose, but they were not. That is the mystery of Mama and Papa. When I look at photographs of the two of them together in the beginning, when Mama, especially, was quite young, and think of how it all turned out, it seems almost impossible. Our house had a splendid dining room with a mahogany table at which twenty guests could eat with their elbows out, though guests were very rare, due, Nurse said, to Mama's nerves. At meals Mama and Papa would observe each other from opposite ends of the long table, and Mama's gray eyes would fly angry silences at Papa, who would catch them in his enormous mustache. Their marriage was a tall column of pain, like a fluted vase. Balanced precariously on the fricative point at which Mama's personality met Papa's chin, it was always about to fall over and smash. I was not encouraged to speak at the table, or maybe I chose not to speak for fear of being the one to knock the vase over. Whatever the reason, when I think of those meals I am struck by the silence: I sit in a carved and gilded chair, in the gulf between my parents and at a great distance from each, arranging my food into islands and oceans and stirring the oceans into whirlpools, while the back of the chair stabs me painfully in the shoulder blades. When I told Clarence about this he said that it sounded like something out of a movie, by which I think he meant sumptuous and posh, but also, perhaps, not quite real. Despite her nerves Mama enjoyed going to parties much more than Papa ever could. Thinking about it now I imagine that her nerves might actually have prompted her to go to parties, in order to relax, if Papa had been getting on them for a while, as despite his best efforts he could not stop himself from doing, in the same way, I imagine, that I could not for the life of me stop myself from getting on Clarence's nerves, and vice versa, that being, I suppose, in a general way the mystery of people being together, being close together in the same house for a long time, though "the same house" in the case of Clarence and me was a series of different houses, one after another over the years, growing bigger and bigger and then smaller and smaller, but always together in them anyway. When we were first together we typed in the same room, at the same table in the place we lived in at the outset, which was my apartment in New York City, but later we typed in different rooms whenever we could, if we had other rooms, and if they weren't too cold, as they were in France. We had a lot of writer and painter friends in those early days. We were convinced that every one of us was going to become famous, though no one ever did except Clarence in a way. The way he became famous was among people who read hunting and adventure stories in magazines and noticed the name of the person who had written them, the same people who later bought his novel. I had written most of one book before I met him but had not shown it to anyone, and then I tried to write another, which was not as complete, though the writing was better, and when I showed parts of that one to people they failed to understand it at all; they wanted to know what I was getting at. When we lived in Philadelphia we typed on different floors, meeting for meals and having friends over or going out every night, and we read to each other what we wrote. I tried to write novels but I could not make them go, though Clarence still read me his, and I made suggestions and typed up what he wrote, and that was the period when I began to rewrite constantly. We told each other that we were in it for the long haul. More and more we talked only about people who were in it for the long haul.

When they brought me to kindergarten that first day—"they" as I said being Nurse and Mama—I took one look at the children, while the numerous heads, which I recollect as being absolutely enormous, swiveled in my direction; swiveled, I want to say, like cannons, though of course people's heads, especially children's heads, don't look anything like cannons. I took one look and threw myself down flat on my back on the floor and screamed, and I did that every day until they gave up. They had formed the idea that I ought to associate with children my own age, supposing this to be good for me in some obscure way; they thought of it as socialization, I imagine, though of course they would not have used that word. They probably hoped kindergarten would improve my character, which was execrable. When I was at home I would lie on my stomach to scream, as I would still, I suppose, were I to lie down and scream today, unless I had been hit by a car, as I nearly was again this morning due to wearing earmuffs in the street, and knocked on my back, in which case I probably would not bother rolling onto my stomach—assuming I still *could* roll onto my stomach after being struck by a car—before starting to scream. I suspect that if I lay flat on my back to scream on the first day of kindergarten it was in order to see the effect I was having on the other children, though now I cannot recall what that was. At the time I had had so little experience with other children that I might have been incapable of even discerning what the effect was exactly, there being, after all, scarcely a whisker's difference, as bare expressions go, between a laughing child and one that is jeering. The only children I saw in those days, before I went away to school in Connecticut, except for an occasional cousin and the ones I glimpsed fleetingly from the car window when Nurse took me out driving, were the small Irish and Italian boys who ventured up the hill to gawk at our house. Those children all had buzz cuts—because of lice, I was told—and their ears stuck out from their heads in a strikingly perpendicular manner. The iron spears of our fence were spaced in such a way that sometimes they got their heads stuck between them, due to the ears, and would stay that way, at times wailing loudly, at others just whimpering, until the gardener could dislodge them by pressing firmly on the top of their heads with a boot, after which they invariably ran off with their hands to their ears. I used to tell people that Papa had designed the fence in that way in order to trap children, but I don't think that was strictly true. It is true, I think, that neither of my parents were fond of children. Send us a chapter, Grossman wrote back, and we'll see. When I read that, I thought, What kind of life has chapters? Clarence sometimes spoke of opening a new chapter. Or maybe it was turning a new leaf.

I would like to go out, get out of this apartment, to the movies or the park. It has been a long time since I have been to the movies, several months, surely, because it was winter. The park is not a green place to stroll about in, as one might think from the fact that they even call it a park—a "pocket park" is how they call it exactly. It is a fenced-in mostly concrete triangle formed where two streets slant together, with a tree, four benches, and flowers in a narrow bed next to the fence on one side; pansies and daffodils now. The locust tree they planted in the fall has not begun to leaf yet. Perhaps it died in the course of the winter. They planted a maple in the same spot two years ago and it died. A honey locust grew by the back gate at my parent's house. It was covered all over, even on the trunk, with long wicked thorns, while the tree in the park has no thorns at all. The shrike, called the butcher-bird, impales its prey on a thorn. It catches insects, lizards, and smaller birds, eats what it can, and leaves the leftovers hanging on a thorn for later. We were looking up at the naked branches of a thorny locust when Clarence told me about the dining habits of the shrike. We were in Missouri. The sidewalk beneath our feet was covered by a thick carpet of tiny yellow leaflets. That was a long time ago. There are no such birds in this park, only sparrows and pigeons. If I go there today I will need to take an umbrella.

Pages and pages ago, when I talked about dragging the type-writer from the closet, I mentioned that the ribbon had dried out—mentioned it and then went on to talk about other things, as I tend to do, and failed to say what I did about it. Not many places still sell typewriter ribbons these days, I discovered; none of the stores in my part of town had a match for my machine, so on the advice of a clerk in one of them I took a bus, two buses in fact, across the river to a district I had never been to before, where there were a lot of low buildings I took to be warehouses, through a part of town entirely inhabited by black people, so that staring out through the rain-blurred windows I thought I was in another country, and then I walked several blocks in the still-drizzling rain to a store the man had said specializes in typewriters. I wondered if he had made a mistake, because when I finally reached the address, I found a little shop that, except for a nineteen-fiftyish looking poster in the display window of a young woman in a pleated skirt and pearl necklace seated at a typewriter, looked from the outside more like an old-fashioned corner grocery than anything else. Beneath the poster a large gray cat was asleep on what appeared to be a folded sweatshirt. I pushed through the door and then just stood there a moment waiting for the man sitting behind the counter to look up from his magazine—an elderly, rather pudgy man, swaddled in a thick sweater. He must have had a shirt on under the sweater with large knobby things in the pockets, as he seemed all lumps and bulges, or else had a terrible disease. When he finally raised his eyes I noticed how tired he looked. He did not have a match for my ribbon, he said after looking at it. The best he could do, he said, was sell me one for a different brand of machine but with the same width as mine, width being all that really matters. I had only to unwind the new ribbon from the spools it came on and rewind it on the spools from my machine, he said. It was not a store, actually, or not a store mainly—mainly it was a typewriter repair shop. A dozen or so machines that people had probably dropped off there to be fixed were lined up on metal shelves against the wall behind the counter, a manila tag at the end of a piece of twisted wire dangling from each. While the man was in back looking for a match for my ribbon, I leaned across the counter, craning, but most of the tags were too high or were facing the wrong way for me to make out the names. I was interested in the names because I don't know anyone who still has a typewriter—has one, that is, in the sense of using it to type on, as opposed to having it lying around in a garage or basement, which I imagine a great many people still do—and I felt a kinship. I was able to read the names on only two of the tags. One was attached to a huge pale-green IBM electric of the sort that toward the end one saw just about everywhere—just about everywhere in offices, that is, not usually in people's houses—not *ever* in people's houses, in my experience. I was struck by just how huge it was. While I might be able to lift it off the ground just barely, I would not be able to carry it up a flight of stairs if I lived on an upper floor. I do live on an upper floor, and what I mean to say is, if I lived on an upper floor *and* I were the owner of such a huge typewriter I would never manage to get it up there, in which case I would want to swap it for something smaller, probably. That would not be terribly difficult, I imagine, IBM typewriters being among the very best, being *considered* among the very best, I should say, since I don't want to suggest that I have had personal experience with them. I suppose I could always just hire somebody strong to carry it up the stairs, if it came to that, though of course it would mean doing the same thing again every time it needed repairs, though being an IBM Selectric that would not happen often, if ever, though on the other hand it obviously does happen occasionally or why was the typewriter here? It was, according to the tag, the property of someone named Henry Poole. When I say I have not had personal experience with this model typewriter, I mean I have not actually typed on one for some considerable length of time, long enough to find out how reliable they really are, but Brodt had one just like it at work that he used for typing up reports at the end of the day, and on a couple of occasions while he was patrolling the upper floors I walked over and typed on his. I had assumed it would be a man's name on the tag, given the magnitude of the machine, though obviously it could just as well have been the name of a strong woman or a woman with a strong, possibly male, friend, or even a friend of just average strength, now that I reflect on it, since they could carry it up the stairs together. Potts and I would be able to carry it up the stairs together, one on each side, as we did the fern, stopping now and then to catch our breath. The other tag I managed to read was attached to a truly ancient machine, a typewriter so obviously antique that I had to wonder if anyone still typed on it, though someone must have now and then, since they had left it to be repaired. The name Underwood was painted across the front in ornate gold script so chipped and worn that if you happened not to remember that this was the name of a once-famous manufacturer of typewriters you would never guess what it said. This machine was the property of someone with a long name that I have now forgotten. It was Poniatowski, I want to say, though that might just be another long name I happen to recall from somewhere. While I was looking at the type-writers and thinking the things I have just mentioned, though obviously not in those exact words, since I was not typing at the time but only thinking vaguely while trying to read the names on the tags, not trying to do that either after a minute or two, just halfheartedly gazing up at them, the man, as I mentioned, was in the back of the store rummaging for a match to my ribbon. I could hear him shifting things around back there. He was not a pleasant-seeming man, but I tried not to dislike him from the outset on account of the typewriters. He was small-eyed and cheeky and had a darting manner that reminded me of a small unpleasant animal, a hamster maybe. He was bald though, which is something one does not expect in a hamster, unless it is a sick one. But he did not look sick, he looked disappointed, which of course many people do, so that is not really a distinguishing trait. A police report, for example, would not bother mentioning it. If you are wanted by the police, how else would you look? Frightened, I suppose.

One would think that just the fact of coming into the store and asking for a typewriter ribbon, an item that scarcely anybody has the slightest use for nowadays, would by itself establish a rapport. I am sure that I for my part was emanating as much warmth as one possibly can emanate during a transaction of that type, even exclaiming "marvelous" several times while he was showing me how to attach the new ribbon to my old spools. I murmured it, actually. I am not an effusive person, just the opposite, and exclaiming "marvelous" exceeds my power. I was, however, because of the typewriters, prepared to become fond of this man, despite the unattractive rodent-like appearance, had he made the least effort in my direction—fond, that is, in the distant way one can become fond of people from whom one buys things on a regular basis. I used to look forward, for example, to buying milk and eggs at my little grocery, because of the large woman at the cash register, whom I have known for years, though I have never in fact said anything to her except sometimes "hello" and "thank you," so perhaps *known* is not the word—when it comes to people obviously *known* is not ever the word. The woman's name is Elvie, something I learned from hearing other people address her in that way, and she grew up on a dairy farm, I once overheard her tell a customer in front of me in the queue. I was expecting something else when I saw the poster in the window and stepped through the door and saw the typewriters with the old-fashioned manila tags dangling from them and the sign on the wall that said We Repair All Models; I was expecting to meet a typewriter person. I studied the man's face while he wrote out my receipt, and I failed to detect even a hint of that. The impression I got was of a bitter, crestfallen man, who was, I had to assume, disappointed with his life. That was to be expected, of course, in someone who had devoted his existence to typewriters, a thing that was now vanishing right before his eyes despite all his efforts to stop it, no doubt taking his life savings with it, his sick wife, medical bills, and so forth, and I did my best to feel sympathetic. After all, I have devoted my own life to typewriters, if not in quite the same way. Still, I had not given up on the man. I asked for two ribbons. I said that I imagined those would last me about a year, and added, making an effort, "See you next year then." I forced a smile. We were typewriter people, after all, how could he fail to see that? I produced, I fear, an ingratiating rictus. "Come here next year, Lady," the man said, "and you'll have to get your hair fixed." He saw my bafflement. I think I reached up and touched my hair, which was straggly due to the wind, straggly and quite gray, with narrow streaks of darker hair still present for some reason. He explained, "It's gonna be a beauty parlor." I felt foolish and stuck my hand in my coat pocket. "You're closing?" I asked. "Closing," he said emphatically. He sounded angry. "Not much demand, I guess." I was still trying. "Horse and buggy." "I beg your pardon?" "Typewriters," he said, "they're like the horse and buggy." I wondered if he had noticed how dirty the windows of his shop had become, though it was only at this point, after I had failed completely in my feeble attempts to like him, that I myself noticed how filthy the whole place was. Even the typewriters on the shelves were coated with dust, as if the people who had left them there were never coming back. I nearly wrote, "Even the typewriters on the shelves were *suddenly* coated with dust," as better capturing the feeling of that moment, the way things had changed abruptly between us, but I feared being misunderstood if I said that. One sees a thing while one is feeling a certain way, and then later, when one has a different feeling, it can look quite otherwise. It can change right in front of your eyes, like something in a magic show. On my down days, when I absolutely have to get out of the apartment, and finally do get out of it, I feel that I am step-ping out onto a different planet from the planet of my good days; even the leaves on the trees are of another color. On the bad days I don't say "hello" or "thank you" to the lady in the market, and I cannot look at her either, she seems so hateful.

The point I am trying to make is that I really *did* notice that the typewriters had suddenly become coated with dust. I asked for two more ribbons. I don't know on what basis I had decided that four were going to be enough. At the time I could not even have said what they would be enough for. I forced all four boxes into my handbag and burst the catch. It had stopped raining, but the wind was cold and blowing straight in my face on the way back to the bus stop. I walked with the handbag clasped in front of my chest. I felt weary, having gone to several stores and ridden two buses already, and I took a taxi home, though I cannot afford to take taxis anymore. In Paris we took taxis everywhere and never thought twice about it. The taxis in those days were mostly old black Citroëns with the passenger door opening forward, making them easy to hop in and out of. If I had to describe my life in Paris in a single phrase it would be "hopping in and out of taxis." That makes it sound as if I led a glamorous life there, when in fact we stayed in Paris for less than a month and I was frantic the whole time.

I was at the kitchen table working on a crossword puzzle. It was just after nine and the city was still loud outside, but it was quieter in the kitchen, away from the street. I had on my gold-rimmed glasses, the ones with narrow rectangular lenses that I used to think of as my reading glasses and that now, since I have stopped reading, I think of as my crossword glasses. I was bent over the puzzle, from time to time tapping my pencil nervously against the edge of the table, I imagine, that being a habit of mine when working crosswords—an annoying habit of mine Clarence liked to say, if he was trying to write and I would tap—when the door buzzer sounded, causing me to jump. I thought, Surely it is Giamatti this time, and I pictured him at the top of my stairs, overweight and rubicund and breathless, but it was Potts again, dressed in shiny black pajamas, barefoot, and looking on the brink of tears. Penned in the rectangle of light falling from my open doorway, she stood with her arms outstretched, palms up—in supplication, I am sure she intended—she is quite devoutly Catholic—though she looked to me like someone waiting to catch a large beach ball. "Edna," she said, "Edna, *dear*. I have to ask a *huge* favor. I feel *awful* about it. You know how awful I feel, and I would never ever bother you if there was anybody else at all." I took off my glasses and she came into focus, looking up at me with liquid basset eyes, hoping against hope for the miraculous descent of a candy-red beach ball. She opened her mouth and closed it. "Favor? I echoed. I might have arched my brows. I don't know. I have a tendency to do that, especially the right brow, but am not always aware that I am doing it. "I cannot imagine a more irritating gesture," Clarence said once in reference to my eyebrows. I would not call it a gesture, though. The word, I think, is supercilious. Potts noticed and blinked. "He's not coming for Nigel," she whimpered. "He *said* he would, but now he's *not*." She dragged the *not* out, flattened it to a thin low wail, then suddenly lurched forward and grabbed my hand in both of hers: "*Help* me, Edna." I was startled and took a step back, jerking my hand from hers. "It's O.K.," I said. I was surprised at how dry and sharp my voice sounded, how supercilious, and I made an effort, softening: "Don't worry," I said, "we'll think of something." I dislike scenes, and I could feel the irritation rising, a burning pressure in my chest. Irritation and embarrassment. I felt constricted and ill at ease. She sat in my typing chair, but barely glanced at the typewriter or at the pages on the table and on the floor, some of them. Her pajamas had silver moons on the cuffs. She had painted her toenails pink. I sat in the armchair, head bowed, hands pressed between my knees, and made an effort to listen. It was about forgiveness and betrayal, friendship and debt, and the politics of rat and mouse clubs; the ramifications were myriad and confusing, but the gist was clear: she had no one to take care of her rat. I got up from the chair and paced. She followed me with her eyes, still talking. I crossed the room to the window. I looked down at the street. I watched the cars. I was straining to listen. I made several small noises, expressing agreement, commiseration, interest, whatever she wanted. After a while, though, I could not anymore, and I drifted off, letting the muffs fall over my ears, metaphorically speaking. The voice at my back flattened, droned, became a radio left on, someone on a telephone in another room, becoming none of my business. I turned abruptly: Potts looked up, startled, and stopped talking. I went over next to where she was seated. I towered over her. I told her I was sorry. I told her I was tired and had to go to bed. She told me she was flying out in the morning, it was her grandson's birthday, her ticket was nonrefundable. I tossed her the ball, and we carried the rat tank up, one at each end. It was not as heavy as the fern, but we had to tilt it going up the stairs, and the rat slid backwards out of its tube. The shavings slid into a heap and buried it. It struggled to get free, kicking off the shavings, which tumbled back over it. It scrambled frantically, climbing up and slipping back down on the glass floor of the tank. Obviously Potts, being shorter, ought to have gone in front. We set the tank down on the floor next to the fern, and the rat scuttled into its tube. Potts lifted the wire lid and smoothed the shavings with her hand, then returned to her place and came back with a pail of food pellets and a garbage bag full of more shavings. She tried to force money on me. I declined, and she left, trailing thanks. I carried the bag and the pail into the kitchen. The rat has emerged from the tube and is standing on its hind legs, forepaws up against the glass, watching me. It is a white-and-black spotted rat. There have been several rats during the decade Potts has lived below me, of various patterns and hues, none of them bright or gay, all in my view faintly repulsive, especially their feet, which are invariably pink and bear an unsettling resemblance to tiny human hands, the hands of tiny humans. They have regularly died after a couple of years, producing copious tears, and a few days later a new rat.

Potts failed to inform me that her rat is a nocturnal creature. I ought to have known it, of course, because of the rats in Mexico: when we lived in Mexico for two months one summer, rats roamed everywhere at night. And I once had lots of noisy nocturnal mice in this place too, until Giamatti sent a man over who put poison everywhere—he even pried loose the baseboards and put poison behind them—and since then I have not seen any mice at all. I am not sure how much I can type today, feeling the way I do. It is the way I used to feel in the months before Potopotawoc, even when the sun was out. Maybe tired is not the word. Empty and wasted are the words. I was almost asleep when it started: a small brittle noise like someone snapping wooden matches, then a dry crunching like someone eating popcorn, then a hollow scraping, then a rustling like dry leaves blown across a sidewalk, then a repetitious creaking like a rusty hinge being worked back and forth, and then a rhythmic swishing like a piece of paper being slid in circles on a floor, that last, I think, being the noise it makes running inside the little yellow wheel. At first I made an effort to assimilate the noise to the wider sounds of the city outside, but it detached itself, insisting *I am here, I am near, I am alive.* I had the bedroom door open as usual, and only a few feet of hallway lay between me and the rat. I very much dislike being shut up in small dark rooms, have disliked it ever since the woman who came after Nurse would lock me in a closet when I screamed, when I had what they, that woman and others, called a screaming fit. Her name was Rasmussen. That was her last name, though it was all anyone ever called her, except my father when he was jolly from drinking, when he called her Rasputin. She possessed an extravagant bosom, very pale hair, a small nose, and a broad pale face that broke out in splotches when she was angry. Nurse had held me in her arms and rocked me when I had a screaming fit, but Rasputin could not stand the sight of me. Even so she did not lock me up for every episode, only for the ones that went on for a long time, hours and hours it seems to me in retrospect, when she must have reached her wits' end. I would lie on the floor, on my stomach, screaming, and she, having lost her wits at last, would rush at me from behind, grab me by a wrist or ankle, and drag me across the floor (I would be clutching at rugs, chairs, etc., as we went) to the nearest closet, and yanking me to my feet, shove me inside, then jam a chair under the doorknob. Sitting on the floor in the pitch-dark, on boots and shoes as often as not, I would batter the door with my feet. One day I kicked so violently I shook the chair loose and escaped into the yard, where I ran shrieking in and out of flowerbeds and hedges until brought down by the gardener beneath a verdant swan. After that she would lean her shoulder against the door, which made me kick even harder, encouraged by the feel of her body on the other side absorbing the impacts through the wood. I would hit and kick the door and throw myself against it and against the walls—and, I recall vividly, against the ceiling also, though that does not seem plausible now—screaming and hurling myself against them, for all the world like a moth in a lampshade. Not like a moth, actually, because moths don't scream, or not in a way that we can hear, though perhaps they make an extremely thin high-pitched wail beyond the range of our hearing, fortunately. How awful it would be if in addition to clicking against the shade and bulb moths made angry high-pitched screaming sounds. If that were the case one could imagine someone saying, "That's Edna in the closet screaming like a moth." Rasputin covered my bruises with face powder afterwards, so people would not notice, and I would wash it off in the bathroom at bedtime and study the bruises in the mirror and feel satisfied.

Just when I was growing accustomed to one of the rat's noises and beginning to drift off to sleep, it would leap to another—abandon crunching, for example, in order to scurry madly. But more iniquitous than the sounds were the intervals between them, when he made not a peep, taunting me with silence instead: I lay there, stretched out on the bed, exasperated and desperate, and waited for him to start up again, waiting, I want to say, *impatiently* for him to start up again. I thought of the rats in Mexico, which had seemed to go about their business in perfect silence, of the solemn way they would look up at me when they paused under the street-light. How dignified, circumspect, and courteous they were, compared to the berserk creature in my living room. After a long while I got up and closed the door. The noise was barely audible then. But with effort I could still hear it, and I could not stop myself from making the effort, and then it was worse than before, owing to the intensity with which I focused on it, with which I was *compelled* to focus on it, now that it had become faint. I thought of Mr. Potts lying in the terminal dark being gnawed by cancer, while next to his bed a rat was chewing. I felt gnawed by cancer. I got up again and dragged my big square window fan out from under the dresser and switched it on, though it was too cold for a fan. I pulled the blanket up over my head and folded the pillow up around my ears like a muff. The scraping and whirrings of the rat, small and vital, vanished at last in the larger whirring, mechanical and electrical, of the fan. The sounds of dead things, by which I mean mechanical and electric things, are seldom as annoying as the sounds living creatures come up with, I have noticed. Snoring, for example, or smacking one's lips while one eats or making little whistling noises while one works, as Clarence did, are just some of the irritating sounds that humans make; and as for animals, there is barking at night and purring while one is trying to think, as well as the various rat and mouse noises I have been discussing. I suppose we cannot help thinking in the case of people and animals that they have come up with the noises for the sole purpose of annoying us. I once threw a glass of water at Clarence to make him stop whistling. And there were the parrots in Venezuela, which were such a torment to him. Despite being awake half the night, I was up at the crack of dawn, and the first thing I saw when I stumbled into the living room was the rat asleep in its tube, its rat tail poking out. I don't know which is more revolting, the little pink hands or that long, hairless, strangely sinister worm. I stared at it lying there, placid and slightly curled, and it occurred to me that it was only pretending to be inert, that any second it was going to whip about. The sun had just come up and I was back at my post, but I was not typing yet—I was drinking coffee and thinking about typing, adumbrating the various items I would want to type up once I got started—when I heard Potts leaving, suitcase thumping down the stairs to the street—thirteen stairs, thirteen thumps—and clicking over the tiles in the vestibule, the street door opening with a faint whang and closing with a sigh and a click. A car door slammed, a car engine became loud, then soft. The morning was very quiet. Today is Sunday. Potts does not in the normal course of things make noises that I can hear from my place, except in winter when she goes down the stairs wearing boots with hard, racketing heels. Even so, now that I know she is gone a different kind of silence has descended on the building; not the silence of no noise, I want to say, the silence of no person. In the back of my mind I must always have been aware that she was somewhere about, just under my feet, busy with her life. And I ought not to have said that a different kind of silence *descended*, when actually it is rising out of the apartment below me, seeping through the floor on which my chair is sitting; rising, I want to say, like smoke. Thinking about the silence down there, I have a mental picture of the aquarium and the fish swimming quietly back and forth, with drifting fins. I wonder if Potts thought to open the curtains before leaving. In my picture the fish are swimming in dense twilight. They can wait until tomorrow for their breakfast.

I slept last night with the door shut and the fan running. This morning I went down and fed the fish and then walked around the block to the other side of the ice cream factory, to the diner for breakfast. Walking that way I sometimes see groups of workers standing in the parking lot, taking a cigarette break, dressed in snowsuits even in the warmest weather, but there was no one this morning. The waitress said she was surprised to see me on a weekday. I told her I was on vacation. After breakfast I walked to the park and sat there, and then I came home and had lunch. I had meant to lie down for a few minutes after lunch but slept half the afternoon instead. The rat has come out of its tube; I can hear it behind me scratching in the shavings. I don't understand why people want to keep rats as pets, or any animal for that matter, except cats and dogs. And parrots, I suppose. When we were in Venezuela we stayed part of the time in a hotel where there were parrots everywhere. They were wild parrots—the hotel put out food to encourage them to hang around in the courtyard and gardens, where they kept up a tremendous racket, such a potpourri of hoots and whistles. I thought it was lovely, but Clarence, who was trying to work the whole time we were there, complained about it to the management, and they promised to try and quiet the birds but of course did nothing. I said, "What do you expect them to do, shoot them?" We were in Venezuela because they were making a movie there. They were working from a script that everyone agreed was atrocious, when the chief writer, whom they all blamed for the problems they were having with the shooting, went off in a huff, leaving Clarence to fix the script up by himself, even though he did not know the first thing about film writing and had only gotten the job because he was a friend of the main writer, the one who left even after Clarence had begged him to stay. I don't recall the name of the movie, or if it even had a name, since it was never finished, but it involved human sacrifice. Clarence was having a terrible time with the script, being obliged to retain all the awful parts they had shot already. The director and the producer, who could see as well as anyone that they were heading for disaster, were in constant dispute over the direction the film should take, and they kept changing their minds, forcing Clarence to rewrite the same scenes over and over. There were no air conditioners in Venezuela in those days, just electric fans, and it was extremely hot. And when the great stone pyramid they had built just for the movie burned to the ground, Clarence had to go back and rework the whole thing once again, taking out the Aztecs and transposing the story to a convent, because there was an abandoned convent near where we were shooting. The pyramid was not made of actual stone, obviously; it was made of wood and covered with canvas painted to look like stone. I sat in the courtyard drinking iced tea and writing letters to everyone I could think of, while Clarence was drinking Scotch in our room, and in between the noise of the parrots—and other birds too, there were a lot of other species of noisy birds—I could hear the tick-tick of his typewriter. More than once, I think even several times during the last week or so, he was seen leaning out the window screaming at the parrots. The electric fans had metal blades in those days, with just the most cursory sort of guard on them and openings big enough to put a fist through. We argued a lot during our stay there, Clarence objecting to my friendships with some of the crew, and I would be talking, trying to explain about the friendships, and Clarence, shirtless and sweating at his desk, would hold a pencil against the fan blade. It made an awful clatter, and of course I would have to cease talking and just wait until he stopped doing that. He was also angry, I am sure, because I would not help him with the script. The truth is I could not have helped him had I wanted to. There are certain types of things I cannot possibly write, cannot, I mean, possibly bring myself to write. All Clarence's class resentments would come out then, when I would have to refuse, and he would accuse me of all sorts of things. He finally did put his fist into the fan, and it chewed his knuckles up. He told people later, when they noticed the scars, that he had done it in a fight. He meant for them to think it was a fistfight, of course. This table is not really suitable for typing—not sturdy enough to withstand the vibrations. Had I known at the time that I would one day be typing again, I would have bought a desk instead. I type, and the pages I have typed already and placed in a neat stack behind the machine jiggle their way across the tabletop, inching millimeter by millimeter (if one can say that) across it until they reach the edge, where they cantilever out, farther and farther out over the edge until they suddenly tip downward and cascade off, as several have just done, one after the other, like lemmings. I could type in the kitchen instead, if I wanted. There is a sturdy table topped with white tiles in there, or I could just move that one into the living room, if I felt up to it. I don't feel up to it. The moving men had to remove the legs to get it in there, and besides, the sun does not rise in the kitchen, cannot be seen rising from that room. I am thinking of moving the rat's cage, into the bathroom perhaps, where I won't have to see the animal constantly. I considered carrying it back down to Potts's place but doubt I could manage that alone. I am not sure where I can put it in the bathroom, unless on top of the laundry hamper. And now I see that I have made Clarence look ridiculous, without intending to, when I described him leaning out the window screaming at the parrots. I suppose some people will wonder about my motives—though he would have looked even more ridiculous had I gone into detail. I did not even mention that while he was doing that, howling out the window and such, he was naked except for a ragged straw hat. The hotel staff would rush into the courtyard and stand in little clusters nudging each other and grinning up at him whenever they heard him start up. He wore the hat day and night, because it was comfortable, he said, though it was really because he did not want people seeing how bald he had become. People who got to know Clarence at that time could not have had the slightest inkling of what he was like before, how extraordinary he was in certain respects. By saying "what he was like before" I have now made it sound as if some dramatic thing happened at some point and after that "he was not his old self," as the saying goes. I suppose some people reading this will think, "Well, before *what* exactly?" Well, in this case, in the case of Clarence, it was before nothing—when I say how extraordinary he was before, I just mean before a dozen more years of being Clarence.

I had a birthday party, and Mama failed to show up. We all stood around a long time, just waiting, and then Papa whispered something angry, making the parlor maid's face redden, and they brought the cake in anyway, and it was an angel food cake. The party was just me and the servants, plus Papa for a few minutes. I refused to blow out the candles, so Nurse blew them out for me, kneeling behind me with her head next to mine as if we were blowing them out together, though I knew that I was not blowing out anything. She explained that Mama was not there because she was caught up in the social whirl. It was, Nurse said, impossible for Mama to get away, no matter how much she wanted to. I must have been quite upset, because I remember that later in my room when Nurse brought me another piece of cake, I just ate the icing off and crumbled the rest and pushed the pieces down into the heat vent. Days later I saw ants going in and out of the vent, and the gardener came up and sprayed something down inside it. When I thought of the social whirl in those days, I pictured an enormous vortex. It looked a lot like the Maelstrom whirlpool in one of my picture books, but instead of swirling water it was made out of swirling people, men and women in evening clothes whirling round and round, arms and legs flailing wildly as they struggled to escape by scrambling up the nearly vertical walls of the vortex in order not to be sucked down into the bottomless hole at the center. Later when I was grown I several times had the same image in nightmares, except then I was the only person in the whirlpool. I think Papa, being a genuine sportsman, was sorry I was not a boy, and Mama also was sorry, and for many years they tried to engender one, but they never engendered anything. I imagine the effort made Papa feel better, but Mama told Nurse that it made her feel pummeled, told her while I was sitting there. Not just Nurse and Mama but other people also were in the habit of talking as if I were not there, because I was a girl, I suppose, or because they thought I was lost in my own world and not taking in what they said. After a few years Mama had had enough, apparently, and began locking the door to her bedroom. Papa, however, being a man and, I imagine, quite virile, had not had enough. After a long while, after many meals with Mama off in the far distance making silence and throwing it at him, while I sat in the middle distance with my head down stirring mashed potatoes into muddy pools, and after he had tried the door many times, whispering hoarsely and rattling the knob, he finally understood that this was a habit she had fallen into, and then he also had had enough; and at those times, having had enough of the one and not of the other, he would retire to the study after supper and drink brandy until his face was red. The study was a comfortable room, a person could sit in it and not have her shoulder blades jabbed, so anyone who wanted to sit anywhere in our house for very long always sat there, except Mama. When Papa drank he sat there a long time, as I recall. It had leather chairs, a leather-topped table, leather-covered books, and a leathery old butler named Peter who stood behind Papa's armchair and poured. Those were all comfortable things, and I suppose they made Papa feel comfortable sitting there, even when he was unhappy, which would be the reason he could sit there for a long time, because he was unhappy but comfortable. We also had a large comfortable dog named Rupert who enjoyed listening to Papa talk even when he,

Papa, was tight and no one else could understand him. But after a while Papa would have enough of the study also, and then, having had enough of one and not of the other, he would stumble back upstairs and beat on Mama's door with his fist. This happened, it seems to me, a great many times, and then one night when it was about to happen again Mama had had enough of that too, and she threatened to shoot him through the door. I don't suppose it really happened as many times as it seems, and it is possible she only threatened to shoot him once, threatened once to shoot him—fill him full of bullets, is what she said—and it only appeared to be happening all the time because it was so frightening. I don't know if this is useful. My bedroom was across the hall from Mama's, and when Papa began hammering on her door, I would think of places to travel, and after he had gone downstairs I would turn on the light and open the little box with the stamps and lay the stamps out on the bed and pretend that they were island countries scattered across the ocean of the bedspread. I would lay them out in different patterns, in a clump like Fiji or strung out in a line like the Marianas, and spend a long time considering the order in which I would visit them. I would imagine the king or president or whoever was pictured on the stamp coming down to the beach with his entourage to welcome me when I landed, and the entourage would include elephants and horses, usually, and I would fall asleep imagining this, and next morning the maid would have to help me retrieve my stamps from the tousled bedcovers.

Sleepless nights filled with wild thoughts, distracted days, typing fitfully, with many long blank spaces. Sometimes I type and think; more often I think without typing, in the armchair or in bed or sitting on a bench in the park. I was not able to fall asleep last night. I lay in bed for hours, staring up at the dark where the ceiling was, eyes locked open, and I thought, This is how I will look when I am dead. I got out of bed, nearly fell out, sitting on the floor for a few minutes first before getting up and going into the living room. Dawn was hours away, and I could hear the rat moving about. When I switched on the light, it lifted its head and looked at me. I tried to imagine that it looked surprised at seeing me in the living room at that hour, but that was difficult: rats don't seem to have much in the way of expressions, except, of course, agony and the like, which all animals can express— even insects can express that. I slid several pages across the floor with my foot, to a spot near the armchair. I sat in the chair and picked them up and read them over to see if they were up to snuff. Finishing a page, I dropped it next to the chair, the way I always used to in the evening, when I would read over the pages I had typed that day. In those days, after reading a page I would let my arm hang out over the side of the chair, dangle out over the floor, still absently clutching the page, while I read through the next, and then just before reaching the bottom of that one I would let the suspended sheet slip from my fingers and whisper slantwise to the floor, lackadaisically, in a gesture of casual disdain, I thought at the time, as opposed to Clarence's frantic way of balling pages up and throwing them at the trash can or making neat self-congratulatory stacks. Sometimes he would yank a page out of the typewriter with such violence he would make the roller shriek and cause me to jump out of my skin. Clarence was always loudly balling up pages, it seems to me. We once had a debate about whether crumpling paper was a useful release of tension, which was his position, or ostentatious self-indulgence, as I maintained. In the end, when he could not think up any more good arguments, he balled up a page and threw it at me. "Up to snuff" was one of my father's favorite expressions. When he let a servant go, it was because that person was not up to snuff, unless of course the servant had been caught stealing and then he would mention that instead; and not only servants—President Roosevelt (that would be Franklin D. Roosevelt) was not up to snuff, because Papa had not approved of his economic schemes. He said the schemes were a load of hooey. And one day Nurse was no longer up to snuff; I don't know why. I was constantly fearful that I would turn out not to be up to snuff, and I am certain Mama was not up to snuff. On the opening day of shooting season when I was ten, it was discovered that she had gone off in the night with a man named Roger Pip, who had used to play golf with Papa. When Papa found the note, which Mama had attached to the collar of his favorite gun dog, he was on the front steps dressed in a brown tweed shooting jacket, which he ruined by tearing off a lapel. After that he must have been truly demoralized, and he took to drinking huge quantities of Scotch instead of brandy. Unfortunately he could not hold his liquor any-more, and after the third drink he would sometimes shout at me, and after the fifth he could not tell which way was up. Six months after Mama fled I was sent away to school, boarding first in a large house with two elderly women and then later in a dormitory with other girls my age. It is not plausible that I actually remember Papa finding the note and tearing his jacket, since when he went shooting he never set out directly from the house in town but always from a lodge somewhere, so in fact I don't know how he found out that Mama was gone—perhaps he came to realize it only gradually, as I did after a while, after she had been gone a long time. The social whirl, as I saw it, had just swallowed her up. It swallowed her up, and after a few years it spit her out again, in San Diego, where she lived with a man named Hanford Wilt until she died. I was nineteen when she died. Every Christmas and every birthday she sent me presents, always jewelry of some sort, and with the presents came a letter, which she would sign "Mama" and in parentheses write "Margaret Wilt," in case I had forgotten who "Mama" was. The letters were typed on blue paper. There was a girl from California at school who told me San Diego had a perfect climate, with only three rainy days a year. It struck me as odd that a person named Margaret Wilt would choose to live in a place with so little rain. Mama was not a good typist, her letters were full of x-ed out words, sometimes whole lines of x's. Not a good mother either, I imagine you are thinking.

The tank is still there, on the floor next to the fern, where Potts and I set it down. If I lean back in my chair, I can peer around the fronds and see the rat moving restlessly about

down there. It scurries this way and that, climbs up on its little metal wheel and climbs down again, digs in the shavings
with its forepaws like a dog, sniffing. Now and then it pauses
and peers out through the glass wall of its enclosure. Its pink
nose twitches. Its actions have a purposeful air, but at the
same time they seem completely pointless. Not utterly
different from mine, I suppose, if someone were to watch me
going here and there in this apartment; a question of scale.
"Edna scurries pointlessly this way and that in her enclosure," the person watching me might write. Brodt, when he
used to watch me roaming about, might have written something of that sort. At some point, after Mama left, they told
Papa I was suffering from nervous agitation. I don't know
who told him, somebody did, and he took me out of the
country, going first to England, to London, where we saw a
very short, very pale doctor with bad teeth who was not
English in the least (he was Russian, possibly; I have an
impression of a Russian-sounding name, and I catch myself
thinking it must have been "Chekhov," because, I suppose,
Chekhov was a Russian doctor also) and then on to Belgium,
where we spent the summer in the countryside south of
Namur, in a hotel made from an eighteenth-century palace.
"We" at that point did not include Papa, who had left us on
the dock in Dover to go look after his business, I think now,
or to go look for Mama, as I imagined at the time. The
woman who succeeded the woman who had followed
Rasputin traveled with us on the boat going over and stayed
with me when Papa left. I called her Nurse also, though she
was not at all like the original, being American, diminutive,

blonde, and not wearing an apron always, and she was more fun and less enveloping than the first Nurse, less comforting in an enveloping sense, as everyone from then on really had to be. She taught me how to play four kinds of solitaire, not including double, which is not solitaire at all and which we played endlessly in the hotel dining room while waiting for lunch. In the flagstone courtyard was a stone dolphin that spit water from its mouth, and they served fish every Friday. I don't eat fish. The hotel was always crowded, thoroughly stuffed with a great many strange people, including a man who walked holding his shoes in his hands, even in the garden, a boy my own age who barked like a dog when spoken to, and a wispy middle-aged woman who on occasion went into the woods and sang "mon coeur est un violon."

I fell asleep on the sofa. I woke up and it was morning. I opened my eyes, then closed them. I dwelled within a while longer, rummaging there for the remnants of sleep. They eluded me. An awareness of things—hardness of sofa, stiffness of legs, emptiness of stomach—forced consciousness upon me, insidious, insistent, irresistible. One more time. Lying on my back, I stared wide-eyed at the ceiling and listened to the traffic building toward rush hour. Whenever I am home the noise of traffic is out there, more or less, sometimes drowned by the noise of the compressors, sometimes drowning the noise of the compressors, not always heard, seldom listened to except at moments like this, on waking, when the mind gropes for bearings, sometimes not telling for a glad moment if that sound is not truly the ocean.

Only on Sundays and in the wee hours of the morning does the roar diminish to where I can pick out the voices of individual vehicles, separate the sad rumble of the old ones from the whistling smooth rush of the new ones or follow the heaviest trucks shifting down octaves on the curving ascent to the Connector. I have moved the fern. I got down almost on my knees, placed my hands on the rim of the pot, buried my face in the fronds (they smelled like a forest after rain), and pushed. Though my feet slipped from under me several times, knees banging the floor, I managed to shove the pot across the room. But unable to see where I was going, I continued pushing until it crashed to a stop against the wall next the bookcase, pitching me forward into the foliage and snapping several fronds. The pot had pushed up the rug as it slid, folding it into large accordion pleats that were now wedged between the pot and the wall and that took all my strength and several hard jerks to pull out. I was leaning over the bookcase, elbows resting on it, catching my breath, when I noticed the dust on top. I had not noticed it before, not recently in any case, because I don't ordinarily hang my head a few inches above the furniture, as I was doing then. My eyesight is fairly good, considering, but not so keen that I can discern from far off something as retiring and minute as dust. It was, I saw, leaning over it, a rather thick coating, a depressing example of how small things accumulate, so I really might have seen it from a distance had I bothered looking in that direction, looking intently, that is, with the goal of seeing, not just gazing aimlessly about as I am bound to do when navigating this way and that in the apartment so as not to crash into things. Desiccated insects caught between windows and storm panes are a second type of depressing small thing that I have noticed accumulating lately. The fact is, I have not been even mildly interested in the bookcase for quite some time now, ever since I stopped reading, and I doubt that I have glanced in its direction, *seeingly* in that direction, even once, except for the time weeks ago when I plunked the stack of new ribbons on top of it, when I was too excited, enchanted by the prospect of typing again at last—*unexpectedly* typing again at last—to notice anything at all. Now that I have noticed the dust I am going to fetch a cloth from the kitchen and wipe it off. Yellow and brown paint flakes accumulating at the foot of the wall on the landing and stairs would be a third. The bookcase is a quite ordinary piece of furniture, not large, made of plywood and veneer. In it I keep the books I expect to read someday along with the ones I have finished reading but have not bothered to put away. Some have been there a long time waiting for me to get around to them. And I keep a few photographs on top, in ornate pewter frames that we bought in Mexico. All the photographs that are not in frames I keep in the letter box, as I think I mentioned. Also on top, between two photographs, is a stack of small flat boxes; those are my typewriter ribbons. I like being able to look up from the armchair or the typewriter and see the stack of ribbons; it gives me confidence that I will be able to keep on typing. I was on the verge of writing, "keep on typing until I finish," when it occurred to me that I am not exactly sure what finishing means or how I will know when it is finished;

I don't even know what *it* is. When I wrote those words I was just thinking in a vague way of getting to the end of whatever this is, even if in the end it is still not complete, "end" in that case meaning just the place where it stops. With the fern out of the way, I can look down at the rat's tank on the floor while I am typing. I begin to type, and the renewed clatter of the keys seems to startle it, and it looks up at me. At other times it clings upside down to the lid of the tank and peers up at me through the wire while making an odd rattling noise with its teeth. Potts says in her note to vary the diet with leftover fruit—not oranges—and grain. I wonder what she imagines I would have in the way of leftover grain. When I leaned over the tank a few moments ago to drop a piece of apple in, forcing it through the wire, the smell nearly knocked me down. I am supposed to change the wood chips regularly. I haven't done that. I am not sure of the procedure, and I don't know what regular is.

At work, when I was still going to work, I spent most of my time underground, in a room adjacent to a parking garage, in a basement, actually, though they did not call it that. They called it "Level B" instead—the way it appeared on the buttons in the elevator—or "the lower level," thinking, I suppose, it sounded more elegant that way, less like a damp place with cobwebs, though it sounded to me like a district in hell, though in fact it was pleasant down there and tranquil most of the time, except at the beginning and end of the day, when the cars roared in and out. They had put me in the shipping room at first, directly across the hall from the cafeteria on the second floor, but the constant clatter of the machines in there, the intrusive chatter of the people working with me, and the collective roar that jumped out of the cafeteria every time someone opened the door proved too much. I did not go up and complain about the noise in the shipping room, but I did, I think, say out loud, in the presence of people standing near me, several times, perhaps saying it louder than I ought, than I would have said it had everything not been so very loud around me, that it was proving too much, and they moved me to the basement. I had half a room down there. The other half belonged to Brodt. They had built a partition across the middle of the room, separating his side from mine. The partition was made of glass, so it was not difficult to keep an eye on what was happening on the other side of the room, even if one could not easily go there. There was no furniture to speak of in my half, just a long Formica-topped table against one wall, a swivel chair, and a mail cart, if a mail cart is furniture. Mine resembled an ordinary shopping caddy but with metal racks instead of a wire basket, and bigger wheels. The door to the whole room was on my half, and Brodt had to pass through that and walk behind where I would be sitting with my back to him, hearing his footsteps, to reach his half, where he had a long table and a chair identical to mine, a filing cabinet, and another taller metal cabinet with padlocked doors. A row of video monitors hung on metal brackets from the wall above his table, and in those he could see everywhere in the building, even inside the elevators. He would spend hours a day just sitting in the chair, a can of Diet Pepsi in one hand, manipulating a bank of switches on the table in front of him. A great many places seemed to need watching, and by fiddling with the switches he could make one or another flash up on a screen. The rat is scratching at the lid of the tank, standing on top of its little wheel and reaching up to pluck at the wire. Brodt was not a tidy person and his table was piled with all manner of stuff—fax machine, telephone, paper punch practically buried under heaps of official documents and forms and security-related catalogues and magazines—especially car magazines—candy wrappers, takeout boxes, and so forth, and shoved off to the side of all that trash, at the very end of the table, the pale-green IBM electric typewriter I mentioned earlier, for typing up reports, I assumed, though he never typed anything while I was present, either because he was ashamed of being a two-finger typist, as I think now, or because he did not want me to see what was in the reports, as I thought at the time. I don't know that there were any reports. Maybe the typewriter was just there. My table, on the other hand, was as bare as the Gobi, except for an hour or so in the morning, when it was heaped with mail. I pulled handfuls of mail from big post-office sacks and tossed them on the table and then walked up and down the length of the table distributing the envelopes among brightly colored plastic totes that I then loaded onto the cart and pushed from office to office. The arrangement of our tables, jammed against opposite walls, meant that Brodt and I worked with our backs to each other, with our backs *facing* each other, I want to say, to capture the feeling I had of his broad back pointing at me constantly, *jutting* assertively in my direction, I might say as well, to capture the intensity of my consciousness of his being there, despite not being able to actually see him unless I turned around in my chair or turned my chair around (it had wheels), which I did not often do. When I did turn I saw only his shoulders and the back of his head. He might have been sleeping for all I knew. Sometimes I could tell he was awake, when a monitor jumped from one spot in the building to another or the soda can rose slowly, absently, in the direction of his mouth, and at other times I knew he had nodded off, when the Pepsi can slipped from his fingers and hit the cement floor with a dull thud and *phfft*, if it was nearly full, or a shallow clatter otherwise. Our room was usually very quiet, the sound would cause us both to jump, and we would turn and nod. In the afternoon there was usually nothing for me to do but wait for four o'clock and time to go home, and I would prop my elbows on the table, rest my chin in my hands, and doze, or I would work a crossword puzzle. Sometimes, if Brodt was out on his rounds, I might turn around and watch his travels on the monitors. I have not, as I said, been to work in several months. Months and months, and all the trees have leaves. I wear plastic clogs now that the days are warm again, so I don't have problems with laces. I have two pairs of clogs, a green and a purple. I like the purple better and seldom wear the green. I wore them with socks on St Patrick's Day, because that was all I had, even though they are not the right green and I did not go anywhere on that day. My earmuffs are green and black. I left the blue ones at work. When I was a child no one wore green or purple shoes. In that way things are better. Potts said it likes to be taken out and allowed to ride on one's shoulder, hinting, I suppose, that I ought to do that. "He loves to ride around up there," she said. "Just set him down and he'll scramble up your pants and sit on your shoulder." Oh, shudder! More pages on the floor.

I seem to be making progress. Yesterday in particular I worked steadily, starting early in the morning, with the sun practically, and not pausing for lunch. When I finally stopped, I took a step back and contemplated the pages, some on the table behind the typewriter, a great many others scattered on the floor, and then I walked to Starbucks. On my way over there, strolling in the warm spring air, I had a sense of "knocking off," a pleasant feeling of being on my way somewhere to "take a break from work," as opposed to my usual aimless wandering. I sat by the window, near a table clustered with chattering young people. I had a latte and a croissant. A dirty bearded man came up to the window and stared at me through the glass while I was eating. I turned my back. When I turned around again he was gone. And after that I walked over to the park and sat awhile, and then I walked home. Whenever I think of taking a walk it is something like this that I have in mind—perhaps just circling the ice cream factory, which occupies an entire block, or strolling to the diner or to Starbucks, sometimes just walking over there without going inside, or trudging the three blocks to the little park and back. Passing a store window I sometimes look over and see someone I don't at first glance recognize; and then I do, suddenly, and think, Mother of God. I don't actually say those words, even to myself—it is more that I experience a shock of recognition and surprise that I might, if there were someone with me when it happens, express in that way. I have been visiting the park more often since the weather turned warm again, walking over at all hours of the day, when the mood strikes me, it is so close, though never after dark, because of the men who are on the benches then, sullen or juiced up when they are not asleep. As a small child I often took long walks with Nurse through the neighborhood beyond the fence of spears, sometimes up our street and around a curve in the road to a park at the very top of the hill, where I was allowed to climb on the monument to the soldiers who had perished in the war—that would be the First World War—Nurse lifting me onto the pedestal and holding me tightly by the ankles while I looked down through a gauze of yellow-brown haze at the midsized industrial city below—row upon row of nearly identical houses running right up to the base of our hill, to where the trees began, and dimly in the smother beyond the houses gigantic tangles of soot-blackened brick and steel, which were the mills and factories, tall brick chimneys rising out of the heaps, where sometimes I saw a burst of orange flame, indicating, Nurse said, that someone had opened the door to a blast furnace. Our house was on the upper slope of the hill, not entirely on top though, and not quite on the park. Nurse told me Papa had wanted us to live quite on the park, but none of the houses there were suitable, while our house, though not on the park, was suitable, being far bigger than

any of the houses up there. The monument to the dead soldiers was a tall granite obelisk in the center of the park, on
the very peak of the hill, and was, Nurse said, four times
taller than Papa. The names of the battles the soldiers had
perished in were inscribed in angular letters on the four sides
of the pedestal: Argonne Forest, Marne, Château-Thierry,
Meuse, and others I have forgotten, the letters cut deep into
the stone. I spent our first visit to the park digging dirt and
moss out of the letters with a hairpin, disturbing small white
insects that rushed out to be killed with the point of the pin.
On other visits we played a game in which I closed my eyes
and pretended I was blind, palpating the grooves with eye-
less fingers in order to guess the letters, and in that way
learned to spell the names of all the battles, though Nurse
could not tell me how to pronounce them. Meuse in particular was baffling. Mama told me "château" was how French
people say "castle," and Château-Thierry in the picture in
my mind got mixed up with the castle in one of my books,
but since the First World War was a thoroughly modern
conflict, it was the wrong picture. Château-Thierry in my
picture was a castle made of pure white stone, like the castle
of Mad King Ludwig, standing on the absolute pinnacle of a
perpendicular mountain so high birds soared below it. It had
conical red-roofed towers with red and blue ribbon-like ban-
ners floating from the finials. It was Papa who told me it was
the wrong picture. A cannon stood next to the monument,
supported by enormous wood-spoked wheels that I was not
to touch because of splinters. The long barrel jutted
obliquely skyward, at its lowest point just inches above my

head, and one day I jumped up and encircled the barrel with my arms, intending to swing there, and it was hot from the sun. Nurse shouted and I let go. She rushed, grabbed my arms and twisted them wrist-up, hurting. "*Now* look," she said, and I looked: my fingers, my palms, and the undersides of my forearms were orange-brown with rust. Clarence was fond of wars and owned a great many books about them. When he was eighteen he had tried to join the army, in order not to get drafted later, he said, but was turned down on medical grounds—he was missing the tip of his right index finger, his father having dropped the hood of a car on it when he was six. It was his trigger finger, is the reason it mattered to them, I suppose, though it did not prevent him from being a perfect shot the rest of his life. Even when his hands shook so badly the ice in his glass rattled, he could still go out in the yard and shoot cans off a tree limb with a pistol. It was a disappointment to him, I think, to be rejected, though he told people it was a lucky break. And once during the period in Philadelphia when we were still undecided·about whether we liked each other after all, he threatened to join the Foreign Legion. He meant this metaphorically, of course.

Two days of drizzling rain. I typed my way through them. And I have moved the rat tank, placing it on top of the bookcase. To clear a space for it I have transferred everything, all the photographs and ribbon boxes, to the sofa until I can think where to put them, and in the process one of the pictures slipped from my grasp, struck the floor, and shattered—the glass covering the picture shattered, not the photograph. The rat watched while I swept it up. It seems interested in what I do. The top of the bookcase is, as I mentioned, layered with dust. I wiped it off with a bath towel, not a proper dust rag but the only thing I could find, before placing the tank there, all my dust rags being dirty, odd as that sounds, and then I sat on the sofa next to the stack of picture frames and carefully wiped each of those. The ribbon boxes, of course, don't have any dust yet, but I wiped them anyway. No sooner had I finished doing this than I noticed the dust on the lower shelves and a gray fuzz as thick as mouse fur on the tops of the books, obvious from where I was seated on the near end of the sofa, an end of the sofa that I don't in the normal course of things sit on. I usually sit on the other, far end, because that end is against a wall that serves as a prop for cushions in case I want to recline, as I often do when I sit on the sofa instead of in the armchair. I moistened the towel and wiped the books one at a time, top and bottom and sides, and placed them on the sofa too, and then I wiped the shelves. The mouse fur formed black cylinders when I wiped it. On the floor they look like droppings.

Still raining this morning, a halfhearted, senseless drizzle of the sort that always makes me depressed and cross. "Her small rather dingy apartment is plunged in despondency and gloom" is how it feels, how the light feels, seeping through the dirty rain-streaked panes. After pushing the fern out of the way, I more or less forgot about it until this morning, when it occurred to me that I ought to water it—reminded by the rain, I suppose. I carried water from the kitchen in the tall glass vase that I used to put flowers in when I had visitors, which would have been before I came to this apartment, as I have not had visitors here to speak of—to speak *to*, I should say, since there have been window washers and plumbers and Potts, of course, and one or two others, briefly, when I was still going to the library, though those petered out rather quickly—I could not find much to say to any of them. I sometimes bring flowers home from the park, but the stems on those are too short for the vase, so it just sits in a kitchen cupboard, good for nothing but pangs. I thought it would make a suitable watering can, but it turned out to have the wrong shape for that: no matter how cautiously I poured a steady trickle ran down the side of the vase and dripped onto the floor. Abandoning caution, I tipped it straight up, but that did not work either—the water rushed out in a single gush, ricocheting off the fronds, and most of it splashed onto the floor again. So I decided to mist instead. I pumped until my fingers ached, emptied the bottle, refilled it, and emptied half of it again, until the fronds were fairly dripping, as if they were in a rain jungle, I was thinking at the time. The pot stands in a wide puddle now, and some of the spray has gone on the wall as well. I should have thought of that before pushing the fern against it. Since I was still holding the bottle, I thought I would spray a window, just to see. I chose one that does not have notes stuck all over it, the center one of the three in front, as I think I mentioned. I did not spray the whole pane—after soaking an area about the size of my head, I stopped and rubbed with my sleeve. The result was a roundish spot slightly cleaner than the rest of the window. Looking out through it as through a porthole, I saw that most of the dirt was on the other side of the glass. The dirt on the inside seems to be mainly finger and palm prints, due to my habit of pressing my hands to the glass when I stand there looking out. I write that, and I get a picture of myself from the outside, as I must appear to someone stopped in the street below: an elderly woman standing at a window staring out, arms raised above her head, palms pressed to the glass.

Typing or just sitting, I often have the radio on, but I don't always hear it. I have it on because it blocks some of the unpleasant noises coming from the outside. But this morning while standing at the porthole, peering across at the ice cream factory, at the concrete walls darkened by rain, I suddenly heard a woman's voice saying, "That was John Coltrane's 'Lush Life.' Next up, the Modern Jazz Quartet and 'Cortege.'" I waited at the window until it started: a vibraphone, pianissimo, alone at first, then joined by the faint tintinnabulation of a triangle—like harness bells, I thought—and, as the pace quickened, by the whispers of brushes on a cymbal, all of it muted, restrained, and melancholy, like the rain, I thought. Clarence owned several jazz recordings, including that one, which we carried with us from place to place, though I don't think he actually cared much for the music and never put a jazz record on unless we had guests. I think he enjoyed the atmosphere of the music and the idea of himself sitting there listening to it and smoking and talking about literature and baseball with people he admired, most of whom I suppose were genuinely fond of that kind of music. I am going to want to say at the outset that Clarence was a sincerely affable person, embarrassingly affable, it seemed to me, when we went to parties and he made a spectacle of himself. In the presence of certain types of people—those with superior intelligence or talent or a great deal of money, the kind of people he could not stop himself from thinking were successful—he would feel intimidated, because of his background, and because he was, even at his pinnacle, only partially successful, and then he would become obnoxious after a few drinks, despite having started out being incredibly affable, where by "incredibly" I mean back-slappingly so. He would do that because even while trying to be affable in that way he was also trying to defend himself, and more often than not he would end up making the kind of loud, incoherent speech that people found so irritating. Oddly enough, as he became more of an American Outdoor Writer he became more British, despite having never really lived in Britain, except, as I think I mentioned, for a few weeks one summer—British in his manner of dress, his pronunciation, even his vocabulary—and the more he drank, the more imperially British he became, until he was slurringly drunk, at which point it was just North Carolina all over again. Clarence, slightly drunk and beginning to hold forth, would notice my disapproving silence and say something like, "You seem thoroughly steamed, old girl." I hated that old girl stuff. Of course he would regret it all afterwards. At times, after a night of showing off, once he had become sober again and I had explained to him what had happened, he would curl up and shudder with remorse—on the floor sometimes or the damp ground, leaves and grass stains all over his jacket when he got up—and whimper with mortification and chagrin. The actual physical hangovers must have been terrific as well.

Sun again. I was at my table to greet it when it rose. I was eating cornflakes, chewing and thinking and staring out the window at the lightening sky above the factory, not seeing it, though, my vision clouded by memory. I suppose one could say that I was staring into the mists of time. I personally would never say that, though Clarence might have. After breakfast I trotted from room to room throwing open windows, and now the breeze—there is a small breeze—can come in the front windows and leave by the back. I am tempted to say that I have created a crosscurrent, but that is not what *crosscurrent* means, and I really ought not to have said that I was *throwing* open the windows, as that gives a picture of someone just flinging up the sashes with a flick of her wrist. It was a struggle to get some of them open, and I had to push up the storm windows as well, which have not been taken off yet. Ditto for the idea that I was trotting from room to room. I don't trot. I put it that way because it seemed to convey the cheerfulness with which I went about it, which would not have come through had I talked about hobbling from room to room and wrestling with the sashes. "She walked with a springing step that belied her advanced years" is more or less how it felt, though maybe that should be "advancing years." With the windows open, there is a lot of noise coming in from the street, and I have put on my muffs. I don't know what possessed me to say that it sounds like the ocean—it never sounds like the ocean. I used to throw breadcrumbs out the window for the sparrows and pigeons but had to stop because of Potts and her husband, who complained about crumbs blowing into their living room. Sometimes I carry crumbs down to the sidewalk in a bag, if I am going down anyway, though I don't usually remember until I am already in the street and happen to notice the birds. The bay windows are the reason I took this apartment in the first place—those and its being on the third floor, facing east, and not seeming expensive at the time, in relation to the money I had then. It is important that I see sunrises if I am going to keep my spirits up, as I believe I have explained already, so it matters what floor I am on. The apartment is in an old brick building that must have been posh at one time. Being just two blocks from the Connector is what made it not expensive, I suppose, because of the traffic noise and the frightening people who live under the overpass, and because of the compressors, and also, I think, because the building is not being kept up, was already not being kept up when I moved here, and that has only gotten worse. The windows have not been washed thoroughly since the young man I gave the TV to was here to clean them. He took the storm windows off and washed them along with the others, and in the fall of that year the same young man returned and put them in again, and I gave him the television. I called Giamatti about the windows again last fall, about how dirty they have become, and he said window washing was a tenant's responsibility, even though it apparently was not my responsibility for the first five or six years I lived here, when someone came every spring and fall to wash them. They would even scrape all my old notes off with a razor blade and never complain. Window washing in those days was treated as such a matter of course that I was not even warned that they would be coming. They just came, in the fullness of time, like the seasons. I would look up, and there peering in a window would be some man on a ladder; I would notice the squeegee and think, "Oh, it must be spring." Now the windows have become so filthy it is a wonder I can keep my spirits up at all. The table I use for eating and now also for typing stands in the center of the bay, as I think I mentioned as well. Or maybe not. With most of my pages on the floor I cannot go back and look and find out what things I have actually mentioned, as opposed to the things I merely considered mentioning, considered in passing, so to speak, and then didn't. Cannot *easily* go back, I mean, as I probably could do it if I really wanted to. I don't bend easily at the knees (I think I have mentioned my knees also), or at the waist either for that matter, so I don't immediately pick the pages up when they fall off and now I have been walking on them. I generally neglect putting numbers on my pages, don't forget so much as find it too tedious to bother, since I seldom remember to stop typing until I am so close to the bottom of the page it is about to fall out of the machine, and then I am usually in the middle of a sentence or in an agony of thought and in no mood to fuss with numbers. If I picked a page up from the floor now, I would not right off the bat know if it was page ten or page thirty. I used to think that one advantage typing had over ordinary unrecorded thinking was that one could go back over a pile of typed stuff and see what was in it. One cannot go over a pile of thought stuff in that way, because there is no pile, just thoughts falling endlessly down a hole, and even when you have managed to haul something up out of the hole you cannot know for sure whether it was down there all along or was something you had merely imagined being down there and had in fact invented while you were hauling. I sometimes wonder, for example, how much I actually remember about Clarence. And now, with all my pages on the floor and there being so many of them and none of them numbered, I can't go back and look in the typed pile either. And it is not even a *pile* of pages, more like a slither or slew—they are spread out all across the floor, as if I had flung them there. *Broadcast*, I think, is the word for that kind of flinging. Contemplating the sheets of paper broadcast across the floor, I think, Well, I am going to have to do something about that, but then I don't do anything about it. Strewn across the floor like that, the pages remind me of my typing days with Clarence, when I used to send one sheet after another to the floor on purpose, as a sign of indifference and disdain, while he was busy numbering his (at center bottom, the numeral bracketed by hyphens) and stacking them neatly next to his machine. When a stack had attained a certain thickness, he would pick it up and heft it, the same way he hefted pistols at a gun show, and sigh. Like Papa, Clarence had faith in accumulation.

I woke up this morning feeling lightheaded. Going down the hall I had to put out a hand to steady myself on the bookcase. I went over and sat in the armchair, where I fell asleep again, and woke up with the sun shining on my face. I dropped food into the tray, pushing the pellets through the wire lid one at a time, so as not to have to lift it, and when they hit the tray some of them bounced out into the shavings. The odor in there is terrific. Droppings are piling up along the edges; it seems to prefer the edges. I said, "Sorry, Nigel," said it out loud, and he looked up as if he understood. It struck me that his eyes are quite intelligent; they have a glittering quality that could be taken for that, though I suppose it would sound odd, in the case of a person, if one were to say, "His eyes glittered with intelligence." I have made coffee and placed it next to the typewriter. The surface of the coffee vibrates each time I strike a key, and the sunlight, reflecting off the trembling liquid, casts bright rippling circles on the ceiling, like water into which a stone has been tossed. I was still quite young, at boarding school, when I learned how to type, and from the first day everyone could see that I excelled at it. I was quite precocious, really, they said, and they were surprised by that, because I was not athletic otherwise, in ways involving the larger muscle groups. I was clumsy and slow at softball, field hockey, and games of that nature. It was the team aspect of those that did me in and made me slow and clumsy, because I wanted to be elsewhere. I typed right through college, becoming faster every year. Had I been a run-of-the-mill typist, I might never have formed the idea of finishing; it would have seemed preposterous, impossibly out of reach at normal speed. Mama had imposed piano lessons practically from infancy, and a line of governesses had followed suit, and I suppose the lessons contributed to my success at typing, though I failed to become a superior pianist, as my heart was not in that either—willfully failed is what they implied, what Mama implied, when Teacher told her. I could strike the right notes most of the time, but I was plodding and timid, is what Teacher said, looking at me fiercely. Not that I dislike music; on the contrary, in the early days, if I knew Clarence was going to be out of the house for a long while, I liked to play records while I typed, Bartok's *Concerto for Orchestra* being a favorite at the time, though now, were I to hear it, I suspect I might not much care for it. I don't have a record player, not one that works, so I can't find out if that is true, and if I try to recall it in my head, I don't hear anything there. I hear a great many things there, actually, but not Bartok's *Concerto for Orchestra.*

Howlings, grindings, and a weird sort of rubberized shuffling, mostly from the traffic outside, along with the throbbing of the compressors, were what I heard just now, when I listened to see if could hear any Bartok, plus the beating of my heart. Back then, when I still liked the *Concerto for Orchestra,* as soon as Clarence left I would close all the windows and doors, turn up the sound, and go into a frenzy. I would start off in the usual way, smoothly and at a normal pace, but as the tempo quickened with the entrance of the brass and upper strings, I would begin to type faster, and I would close my eyes, and I couldn't hear the typewriter then, but I could feel it shuddering beneath my fingers, and I would commence to sway in my chair. After a minute or two of that a ribbon of words would sometimes start to stream out of the music onto the page, trickle at first and then stream, and I would let go, let myself fall into the music, and it was like falling from somewhere high with no fear of striking bottom, and I would abandon myself to it, turning slowly head over heals as I tumbled, and I felt as if my fingers were tools the music was using to write what it wanted—the music or the machine, I was not sure which— that the typewriter had become the tongue of my hands, not of my brain, and I was unburdened by reflection. Among the incidents in my early life with Clarence that I find most portentous were the times he contrived to walk in on me in the midst of one of those sessions. I don't suppose he did it on purpose, he just stumbled in without thinking that it mattered, and I say contrived because that was how it felt at the time. With the music clamoring wildly, the typewriter thundering beneath my fingers, my back turned to the door, and my eyes closed, I would have no inkling he was there until he flicked off the record player—brutally flicked it off, was how *that* felt. Clarence and I did not have the same taste in music. He just did not have it in him to respond with understanding when I said, "Look, it's Bartok, it's *all* Bartok," and handed him a dozen pages of gibberish. He just glanced at it and then walked around the house opening windows. Had he paused to think, he might have tiptoed up and touched me gently on the shoulder—that would have been startling enough—or he might have withdrawn discretely, taken a seat on the steps outside, or on the swing under the oak in the place in Connecticut where we had one of those, and waited until he could hear that I had finished. It was gibberish to him, is what I mean.

More pages on the floor. They cascade off at the slightest provocation. Maybe the table is slanted, the legs on one side shorter than on the other. I don't know. I bought it used, it was quite cheap, and that might have been the reason. The people selling it probably assumed I was not going to notice until it was too late, assumed correctly, as it turns out, though I cannot assert in a factual way that I have noticed even now—I am merely guessing it *might* be slanted, as an explanation for why my pages keep sliding off without being nudged by anything that I can see, even something not at all obvious, a draft from an open window, for example, or the minute breeze I stir up removing a jacket or opening a closet door. I sit in my armchair, scarcely breathing, windows shut tight, no fan running, and still they fall off, striking the floor with a small dry rattle, which, though I really ought to expect it by now, never fails to startle me. That I have not noticed the slant, if there is one, probably means I have astigmatism. Or, equally plausible, the table is as it should be, all four legs are of equal length, I don't have astigmatism, but the floor is slanted. If I had a marble, I could roll it and see.

Brodt wore brown trousers, a brown shirt with an American flag on the sleeve and the word "Brodt" in white script on the flap of a breast pocket, and black shoes. The writing on the shirt pocket is the reason I think of him as Brodt, as we were never introduced in the proper way. When I showed up for work the first day he did not glance up from his monitors, and after that of course there was no point. Well, perhaps there was still a point, but the possibility had slipped away. If one has failed to say, "Hello, my name is so and so," right off the bat, it becomes impossibly awkward to go back and remedy it later. I never learned his first name, unless of course Brodt was his first name. In fact Brodt probably was his first name, since the man who came to empty our wastebaskets had "Larry" on his pocket. Brodt was not a communicative person; "a phlegmatic and awkwardly taciturn man" is how I might begin to describe him, were I writing a story. I never saw him excited or even slightly animated, except once a few years ago at the time of the explosion of the airplanes in New York. They had moved a television into the cafeteria, they were crowding around it, and I could see Brodt standing in front of everyone waving his arms and shouting. He *looked* like he was shouting at any rate. I saw him on a monitor, gesticulating, and he looked like the angry cop in one of Chaplin's silent movies. When he left the basement room it was usually to stroll about in the lobby, make the rounds of the offices, go to lunch in the cafeteria on the second floor or the bathroom on the first, or eject someone from an office, if that person had refused to leave for some reason. When he left the room I could turn my chair around and watch his travels on the monitors. To get out of the room he had to open the small door in the partition and walk across my half, behind where I would be sitting or sometimes standing, to the larger door that opened into the garage. Now and then, when he was crossing behind me, I would hear his footsteps slowing, or even stopping, rarely. I could feel him peering over my shoulder, checking on my progress on a puzzle, and I would picture him fighting back a temptation to make a suggestion. He never did make a suggestion, and I never turned around at those times and never looked at him from anywhere but behind or saw anything but the back of his shoulders and head when he was in his chair. I glimpsed him from the front only when he got in my way, when I was trying to go someplace or other in the building and he was standing in the middle of the hall, obliging me to walk around him, or when his soda can fell and caused us both to swivel, as I mentioned. Now and then, if we were waiting at the bus stop together after work, I looked at him from the side and took the measure of his profile: low, back-sloping forehead, bulbous potato nose, rounded chin, barrel chest, protruding stomach, and so forth. He never talked to me, except occasionally when we were at the bus stop. I am not sure he was talking to me then either, as he did not turn his head in my direction when he talked, and I was careful not to turn mine in his, so as not to seem prying in case he wasn't talking to me after all, and what with the noise of the crowd and buses and the fact that I was not facing him and often had my muffs on, I seldom caught more than a stray word or two. I had worked there for quite a long time before I went over and typed on his machine. Every morning and every afternoon he left the room to carry out his inspections and patrols. I could see him going from place to place on the upper floors and was not worried that he was going to walk in on me while I was typing. It seems strange that the only place in the whole enormous building where I was sure he was not watching me was in his own office. Though it is not odd if you think about it—the eye, after all, can't see itself. I was not interested in typing anything protracted and did not sit down to do it. I went over and typed on his machine twice. The first time I wrote, "Why don't you speak to me?" The second time, a few weeks later, I wrote, "Hello. Hello. Hello." One day, a few months after that, I bought him a book at Barnes & Noble. I bought *Winesburg, Ohio* and placed it on his table while he was out. It sat there for weeks, until I went over and took it back. I seem to be making headway. "Edna is inching her way forward at last" is how it feels exactly. I like the word "headway," one of those nautical terms we use all the time without ever thinking about their actual meaning—headway, movement ahead, as opposed to leeway, drift to the side. Toward the end, when Clarence had developed such a short fuse, I remember sitting at the breakfast table talking to him about something or other and having him suddenly slam a fist down on the table with such force the coffee in our cups sloshed into the saucers and shout, "*Will you get to the damn point!*" That happened, as I said, toward the end, and that, meaning the end of Clarence, is another item I am going to have to type up at some point, at some point before the end of this. Drift to the side is a problem, obviously.

"Losing one's bearings" is another interesting phrase of that sort. Clarence and I once had a dispute about that phrase, he thinking it meant losing one's *ball* bearings, until I showed him in a dictionary. He thought this, I imagine, because of growing up the way he had, with dismantled cars lying around in the yard. He told me there were always broken cars in the yard, several at a time, because once a car had broken down definitively there was nowhere else to put it, and of course ball bearings would have been falling out everywhere. He told me they used ball bearings as ammunition in slingshots, when they hunted squirrels and rabbits in that way. There was never a question of headway before I started typing again this time, no question of reaching a conclusion or finding a solution or anything of that sort, reaching a point, I mean, where I could stop turning things over; getting someplace was not the aim. If there was an aim in recent years, it was, as I said, just to pass the time until four o'clock, when I could go home, even though when I got there it was to go on doing the same thing, sorting and putting in piles, but doing it in the brown armchair. Maybe "thinking" is not the word for that; "woolgathering" is better. Of course if one keeps at it and continues drifting to the side long enough, or gathers too much wool, one can end up losing one's bearings, losing them in a fairly agreeable way, possibly, and losing them *temporarily*, usually, I should emphasize, as opposed to losing one's mind for good or being tormented by some terrible thought forever, some awful unshakable memory perhaps, or being actually lost at sea. "Willy-nilly" would be another way of describing how my thoughts came and went, wafting this way and that. In a sense I really was lost at sea, had got accustomed to just drifting, blown this way and that by the winds of velleity and memory, making it hard for me to push forward now that I am typing again. With the windows open wide, as they are now, and a rain-freshened breeze blowing in, I could almost be typing on a balcony. I hear sparrows chirping on the sidewalk, even over the noise of the ice cream machinery and the cars. This morning I took some half-stale bread from the kitchen and crumbled it as best I could—it was not quite stale enough to make genuine crumbs—and threw it out the window.

I have placed a book on top of my pages, the ones I have stacked behind the machine, to stop them from sliding off the table. I chose the first book at hand, just grabbing it from the bookcase in the hall on my way into the living room this morning. It turned out to be Peter Handke's *The Weight of the World,* a book I remember liking quite a lot at one time, as it seemed to be saying many of the things I was thinking then, and the title now seems weirdly fitting, considering its new work as a paperweight. I am always startled and thrilled by coincidences like that—startled awake, even though, before they occur, I am not aware of being asleep. For a number of years, when I was much younger, I practiced eliminating causation from my world-view, in favor of coincidence, in order to wake up. The aim was to turn every moment of experience into an amazing accident, in order to break through the film of complacency and habit that I could, even at that young age, feel shutting me out from actual life, or from what I considered actual life at the time, like a glass pane placed between me and the world, something, though on a more spiritual level, rather like the plastic film that makes the things wrapped up in the supermarket appear so remote and dead. I worked at it quite hard for a time, and I reached a point in my practice where preparing coffee in the morning I would tip the kettle and be astonished that water came from the spout and that it poured down into the filter rather than up toward the ceiling—happily astonished, I should say. In fact I was only pretending to be astonished. I knew all along that the water was not going to fly up to the ceiling, even while I was assuring Clarence that it might. I would speak to Clarence, perhaps interrupting him at his work, and he would respond, maybe, and if his response had any bearing at all on what I had just said, I considered it a lucky break. Clarence said, when I was practicing all the time, that no one could live like that systematically. I told him there were no systems, only piles of accidents, that everything that is not strange is invisible. I think Valéry said that, or something like that. I didn't tell Clarence that Valéry had said it, though, because it annoyed him when I quoted French authors. But after a while I got tired of the whole thing and went back to seeing the world as the same old place, worn by familiarity and habit almost too smooth to feel.

The butler died and no one replaced him, the gardener was let go, the animals in the hedges vanished into thickets of unpruned branches, pine trees and oaks sprouted from the flowerbeds. Schoolboys kept the lawns more or less mowed, and my father could still spend hours out there whacking at golf balls in all sorts of weather. I could hear the whacks from inside the house, on and on, a row of sharp cracks like rifle fire, a long silence while he walked to the end of the lawn and picked up the balls, and then more whacks when he knocked them back the other way. Sometimes a ball crashed against the side of the house or sailed through a window-pane. Papa really didn't care about broken windows, and if the weather was warm he just left them that way, and at night insects swarmed through the holes and buzzed in desperate circles around the lamps—sometimes it was impossible to sleep because of the mosquitoes inside the house. In winter he blocked the holes with pieces of corrugated cardboard, but he never bothered doing that in summer, despite the insects, and one of the first things I would do on my visits home was walk through the house, count the holes, and hire someone to fix them. The iron fence did not receive a fresh coat of shiny black paint in the spring as before and turned brown with rust, staining my clothes if I brushed against it. The tips of Papa's beautiful mustache, which in younger days had jutted like tusks, hung limply down the sides of his pendulous jowls. Not just his face, his whole body expanded and settled downward like sand in a sack—he became big-bottomed and florid and hitched his pants when he walked.

When the roof began to leak, he sold off the slate shingles and replaced them with rolled asphalt. He had a partition built across the staircase, to save on heat, and slept in the study downstairs. Splotches of mildew blackened the wallpaper. I was young, I was trying to step forth, and all around me were deterioration and decay. I went home less and less often, and when I did go Papa seemed perplexed, and I wasn't always convinced that he knew who I was. Knew at first blush, that is—he always figured it out once we got talking. His sense of humor grew unstable as well, unhinged practically, veering from hearty and vulgar to bizarre and gnomic at the drop of a hat. He tended to lag a few paces behind me when we went out for a walk, and I could hear him back there chuckling. He began to employ the self-referencing third person, speaking of himself as "this one"— "this one," he would say, "is going to fix himself a gin and tonic"—and he would address me as "you one." I am not sure that he did this to be funny. He became belligerent when people failed to get one of his jokes, and almost no one ever got any of them, since they rarely made sense. One day we were thrown out of a restaurant in Philadelphia because he was shouting at a man who had failed in that regard. I spent my days there reading or making meals for Papa or just wandering about in the garden. I liked it better now that it was in ruins. I slept on a sofa in the drawing room, and my father's gigantic snores flew out of the study and mingled there with the buzzing of the insects. Had I been a child still, I might have floated off somewhere, to one of the countries I discovered on my stamps. Instead, I lay shackled to the sofa, rigid with anxiety, and pressed cushions to my ears against the unrelenting assault of Papa's snores (I had not discovered earmuffs yet). At times I became completely frantic, and then I would escape to the bathroom and type until morning. I think that was when I learned to use a typewriter in this way—so as not to become frantic. It is easier not to feel alone when one is typing, even in the presence of the desolation of the *Concerto for Orchestra*. If this were a book with chapters, I would call this one "The Desolation of my Father Snoring."

A fish was floating on its side, one of three orange fish, all the others being red and white. It had a long gray tail and was thoroughly dead. They all have long tails, and it *used* to be an orange fish, I ought to say, it being now pasty white and coming apart in the water, dissolving or fraying, except for the tail, which was unchanged in death, like our hair and toenails, they say. I had not been down there for several days, so I don't know when it died, or of course why it died—not of hunger, I am sure. I lifted it out with a slotted spoon and flushed it down the toilet, and then I fed the others. I was still in college when my father died. Mama was also dead by then, though I don't know if he knew that, as we never talked about her. He died suddenly one day while I was off at school of what I try always to think of as apoplexy, that sounding Victorian and dignified, rather than what it really was, acute myocardial infarction, which sounds perfectly heartless, nasty, and alone, sprawled on the bathroom tiles for three days before they found him.

Myocardial infarction was the proximate cause, I ought to say, since in an overriding and actual fashion he died of an excess of drink. The house was sold, the debts were paid, and there was not a lot of money left over—not a lot, I mean, by the standards I had grown up with, though there was quite a lot by the standards of someone like Clarence, who had grown up with nothing—that might, I think, be the really fundamental difference between us. I spent a big piece of it in just three years, traveling to Europe and living in a nice apartment in New York, with big windows and pigeons on the balcony, before I met Clarence, and then a lot more of it afterwards, when we spent it together trying to be professional writers instead of working. After more than half of it was already gone I put the remainder in investments that were supposed to make it grow, on the advice of a man who had been an associate of Papa's, but it never did grow—it did the opposite, did it quite slowly, though, so I didn't notice the shrinking day by day but only after a number of years, by which time it had already shrunk. That was probably because, as I learned later, the man had only hunted quail with Papa, was not in business at all, and actually made his money painting pictures of racehorses. The fact that it then continued to shrink made Clarence desperate, and he was constantly after me to do something, but I did not do anything, since there always seemed to be enough for us to get by on if only we cut back a little. These days I tend to think of myself as impoverished. I tend to think it especially, even to the point of dwelling on it, when I happen to be feeling down for some other reason, because the milk has turned, for example, and at such times I have even said to people that I am impoverished. Potts, who offered to lend me money, was someone I once said it to. I am not strictly impoverished, in that I am not flat broke, except occasionally toward the end of the month if I have been rash. With four suppers at the diner, two trips to Starbucks for coffee and pastry, and a taxi ride back from the center, due to a large bag of groceries, I have already been rash this month and it has scarcely begun, and of course there is still the matter of the rent, or perhaps I should say the *question* of the rent, it having become questionable, having not been paid in full this month or the month before either. Instead of impoverished, I ought to say "in straitened circumstances," though of course I actually will be impoverished in a few weeks, because of having been rash in the ways I just mentioned. I thought for a while that if this became a book I would call it *Poor People*, but I have decided against it, as that by itself, without explanation, gives a wrong impression: Clarence and I were never poor in the sense of living in a tarpaper shack and eating off tin plates. I was thinking of poor in the larger sense, as members of poor suffering humanity. I typed that and turned and the rat was looking at me, standing up against the glass and swaying back and forth, like Clarence in a doorway after a night on the town, holding on to the doorframe, I was thinking. I am finding its presence annoying and burdensome. After Papa died, I went to France for the first time as a grown-up. Most people I knew traveled by boat in those days; I went on the *Ile de France* with a friend named Rosaline Schlossberg. We had planned to spend the whole summer together but quarreled our first week in Paris, and she went on to London by herself and from there spread all sorts of rumors. She was not a friend in the strict sense, just an acquaintance; Clarence was my only friend in the strict sense. I imagine some people will prefer that I say something on the order of Clarence was the love of my life. I could just as well say that he was the boredom of my life, the annoyance of my life, the chief obstacle to higher things of my life, and so forth. I can say, sincerely, that he was the person I most enjoyed typing with, on many different machines.

I am quite fond of the machine I type on now, have been fond of it ever since I bought it, at a store on Lafayette Street in New York just a month or so before moving to this apart-ment, even though I had already made up my mind to move and a typewriter was going to be just an extra thing to carry. I came here and got a job—not the one I recently stopped going to but the one before that—in a grocery store. That was the first time I had worked in the normal sense—in the pecuniary sense, I should say, since it did not feel normal to me. Obviously I had expected circumstances to turn out differently: I would not have bought a new machine just to type up a few letters and then stick it in the closet. I had owned a whole series of machines in the past but never enjoyed typing on them as much as on this one. It is a fairly big typewriter—I would describe it as a smaller office-type machine—made by Royal, and it emits a muffled yet solid-sounding thud when I strike it, as opposed to the cheap, tinny clatter the little ones make. A person need only hear the noise of the little machines, as I did constantly when Clarence used to type in our room at all hours, to be convinced that nothing worthwhile could possibly come out of one of those, though of course sometimes something actually does. When I say Clarence used to type at all hours, I am thinking of the habit he developed in the middle years of writing after he had taken too much to drink. We went to a lot of house parties back then, where there were hordes of clever people standing around. Clarence would get fired up by the clever conversations, and by the time we got back to our room he had usually convinced himself that he was hard on the track of something tremendously clever and beautiful. He would be terrifically impressed by the witty things he had found himself saying at the party and absolutely had to set it all down on paper right then and there for fear it would slip away while he slept. He would plant himself in front of that awful little Olivetti, as often as not standing in his underwear at the dresser, and clatter away while I was trying to sleep, now and then pausing to read over what he had written. He always approved of what he wrote in those states; I could hear him whispering plaudits to himself— "beautiful," "fantastic," "that'll show 'em." Thank goodness I had usually drunk quite a lot myself, as I regularly did in those days, and I would manage to fall asleep after a while and not wake up until the clatter stopped, startled awake by the silence or by the shaking of the bed when he finally tumbled into it, gray light of dawn at the window. Naturally he would find out the next day that what he had written in that state was not at all the stupendous thing he had imagined—it often did not even make sense, or it made sense but was trite or derivative or some other equally bad thing, and then he would be more depressed than ever. Of course feeling that way just made him want to go to more parties, even though I kept telling him we should get a place in the country somewhere and forget about those people, take walks every day over hill and dale and keep regular hours and drink less. I thought that if he could just forget for a while about becoming famous and start over from scratch, he would be all right. But of course he could not do that, because he knew in his heart that he was not all right. And then when we finally did do it, the regular hours, long walks, the whole kit and caboodle, really, it turned out to be a catastrophe—well, not a catastrophe, properly speaking; it turned out to be a letdown, at a time when we could not stand another letdown. Clarence wanted achievement as a writer, arrival at some recognized state of attainment, more than anything else in the world, except later perhaps whiskey, and later still whiskey and Lily, and for him that meant commercial success at least in a modest way and respect as a professional writer, from other professional writers, and it meant acting like a writer and doing writerly things like correcting proofs and attending publication parties of other writers whom we scarcely knew and who, when we crossed them on the street, failed even to nod in our direction. He was always peering over his own shoulder while he typed, wondering and worrying—and, toward the end, despairing—about what other people, especially people in the book business and later the movie business, were going to say about it. His idea of attainment was to eat in a restaurant in the Hamptons and overhear someone at another table whispering that the man sitting with the odd-looking woman over there was the writer Clarence Morton. I understood that this was an inherited disease of his, one he had brought with him out of his background, from having been born nobody and brought up among people who were always using the word "successful," that it was not just an attitude he one day decided to have, and that that was why he was never able to rid himself of it, even though when we were first together I was confident that he could. He was capable of describing some person he had just met at one of those parties of his, after I had stopped going to them, as "a successful writer" or as having made "a successful movie." I always objected to that way of talking, but I don't believe he ever understood—he would give me a baffled look and say something idiotic like "What have you got against success?" There was, of course, no point in answering. Disgust, actually, was the reason I stopped going to those parties. And turning to me, someone would say, "And you, Edna, do you write also?" And I would say, "No. I type." After he was writing regularly for magazines and after he wrote *The Forest at Night,* he truly was a successful professional writer, but he was not able to value it anymore. He could not value it because of me, possibly, because he knew that I did not place any value on it. So in our life together it became a question of which he was going to value, himself or me, and he could not make up his mind until he met Lily. With her, who did not value anything that I valued, he was able to break free and become himself again, though by then it was too late for that too. If I were feeling ironic, I would call my book *How to Write Like a Pro*. And I have to do something about the rat's chips; I cannot just keep adding more on top. The tank is half full of them already, and it has made tunnels against the glass like an ant farm. A rat farm.

When I was talking earlier about the reasons I might stop typing—the need to ruminate and the desire to go do something else for a while—I forgot about key-jams. I never used to have them, and now there is one practically every day and at the worst possible moment, when I am least inclined to stop typing. I have not mentioned them until now because they are hard to talk about without seeming to complain. At times I become caught up in typing, so thoroughly in the throes of it that my thoughts run faster than my fingers can fly, they pile one on top of the other, and when a great many thoughts are making a racket in my head at once, I can falter, my fingers trip and stumble, and there are spasms: keys collide, pile up, and jam into a frightful tangle. To free the keys I have only to pry them up with my fingers, top key first and so forth—not difficult and scarcely worth mentioning were that the end of it. But that is not the end of it. After prying the keys up, my fingertips are stained with ink, and I have to get up from the table and trundle to the kitchen or bathroom. And there I cannot just stick my hand under the faucet—ink is not dust. I have to wait, tapping a foot or whistling irritably, possibly, until the water runs hot (it comes up from the basement and takes a long time), scrub my fingers, and then dry them on a towel, assuming there even is a towel, which I have just discovered there is not at present, the last clean one having gone for a dust rag, as I think I mentioned, or wipe them on my dress, as I have just done, or pants, or wave them in the air, pacing. Key-jams are maddening. One wants to flail the typewriter with one's fists or even pitch it across the room as Clarence did once, and I do sometimes hammer the carriage with my forehead, though I know that does no good at all, except of course psychologically. He did not throw the typewriter because of a key-jam; he threw it because he had decided he was never going to write again, at least that is what he was shouting when he hurled it. He threw it another time as well, but the reason then also had nothing to do with key-jams or even with typewriters. He did not throw the same typewriter both times, as the one he threw the first time was thoroughly ruined and could not be thrown a second time, except of course in the trash. It was my typewriter he threw the second time, and he didn't break it, since he threw it onto the bed. It occurs to me that people under the age of about thirty probably have no idea what a key-jam even looks like. If this ever becomes a book I am going to have to explain how typewriters work, and the book can include a picture of a typewriter with a little insert showing a close-up of a key-jam, to help them understand. At Potopotawoc they took away my typewriter. I had sent my luggage on ahead, and when I arrived my suitcases were lined up next to the cot in my cabin, but the typewriter was not among them. They told me it had become lost in transit, that they would get me another, but they did not. Then two weeks later I saw it in the director's office. I was walking past, his door was open, and I spotted it on the floor beneath a chair. He said it had just arrived, but I didn't believe him. The Peter Handke book has jiggled off as well, taking several of my pages with it, hitting the floor with a loud slap that made me jump. There are now a great many pages on the floor. You cannot, I suppose, call it a farm if there is just one animal.

Possibly I am not making headway at all. I might even be falling behind. Life is still going on, is the problem. Not going on in a big way, but going on nonetheless, a little bit at a time. Chugging along, I suppose, is pretty much what it is doing, or inching forward, as I suggested earlier. Almost nothing is happening, in the full sense of happening, yet I find that I am not able to process even that little bit fast enough to keep up, despite being a better-than-average typist. I seem to be falling farther behind every second. Here I am wanting to type about things that happened fifty years ago, while Lily and the yellow-papered house and France in winter and so forth are panting in the wings, waiting to get processed, and a picture frame gets broken, and I am compelled to talk about that and about key-jams and dust and so forth, and when is it ever going to stop?

In college I typed things for other people. They asked me and I did it without complaining. It gave me status, I suppose, though I don't recall caring about status, so that was probably not the reason—I enjoyed typing even then. And I fixed the punctuation and grammar as I went along, and the spelling too, of course. Correct grammar came to me as naturally as breathing, because of my background, my social class and whatnot, while it was extremely difficult for some of the others. I had only to say a sentence out loud in order to hear if it was all right, while they had to memorize rules, and even when they managed to write correctly, which some of them did after a time, after I had pointed out this and that and explained, I could tell just from the style that they were writing to rules. Even Clarence would stumble in this way, because of his background. He had a hard time recognizing that something had gone wrong with one of his sentences, just as he would not always notice when something was trite or derivative. He used to bring me things he wanted retyped, his own typing being so slow, clumsy, and completely inaccurate, to let me type it correctly and fix up the grammar. And sometimes I went a little further than that, than just striking out the worst and tidying up the rest, grammatically speaking. I sometimes changed quite a lot of it, changed quite a lot of it extensively. I told him that all the words he had *meant* to write were still there, but now his intentions were clearer. Of course he saw what I was doing, though he never asked me to do it, and we never discussed it. He never said, "Can you fix this, can you make it better, Edna?" It was always, "Can you type this up, old girl?" When he shouted at me about getting to the point, after he had developed the short fuse I mentioned, he had already taken up with Lily— taken up with her after-hours in the pharmacy, not taken up with her in public yet. Lily typed using two fingers. Of course that scarcely mattered, since Clarence had given up writing by then. At some point I am going to have to explain about Lily and the pharmacy, and I have still not gone into Potopotawoc, and that by itself will strike some people as odd. If Clarence were reading this it would strike him as odd, I am sure—odd and, to use one of his favorite phrases, entirely symptomatic. And now I am getting sidetracked, which is another interesting expression, but one that I am not going to go into here, unless I decide to talk about trains, which I have in the back of my mind to do at some point. I ought to say sidetracked *again*, as the sad fact is I am barely making headway, even without Lily and the pharmacy. And if I want to lie down on the sofa again, I will have to move the stuff I piled there, the books and photos and such, and the boxes of ribbons. I have not been wanting to lie down as often as I used to a few weeks ago, when I was spending most of the day horizontal. I could lie down in the bedroom, of course, if I felt like it, or on the rug next to the table, as I used to do sometimes also. I might not want to lie down on the rug now, because of the trash on the floor, the completed pages that have slid off the table as well as a large number of crumpled ones that I tore out of the machine and threw there and haven't mentioned for fear of sounding discouraged, plus the fronds that snapped off the fern while I was pushing it against the wall, and some of Nigel's pellets that have spilled regularly while I was carrying them in my hand from the bag in the kitchen, and Peter Handke's book, and the difficulty of getting back up once I am down there. And I ought to have mentioned before that when I say floor I mean rug as well; most of my pages are on the rug. I think, Well, I need to tidy up, and then I don't.

I have put the books that were on the sofa back in the small bookcase. They were not many. I keep most of my books on the tall shelves in the hall. The door to the kitchen is at the far end of the hall—not a door, strictly, just an open doorway. Standing in the living room one can see all the way through the apartment and out the rear window, though there is nothing to see out there but the iron railing of my fire escape and the back of a brick building across the alley that used to be a school but has been abandoned for years, windows boarded up. Nothing to see, that is, in terms of animate things like people and trees, but the kitchen window faces west, and so it frames sunsets in part, as I might have mentioned, frames part of a sunset, the remainder being blocked off by the schoolhouse. On one side of the hall is the door to my bedroom, and with the exception of that door and the doorway to the kitchen the hall is lined with bookshelves from floor to ceiling and even across the tops of the doorframes. Getting a carpenter in to build the shelves was almost the first thing I did after moving here. Going to and fro in the course of the day, in and out of the kitchen and the bathroom, which is off the kitchen, I have to walk past the bookshelves, though I don't ordinarily look at the books then, in the normal way one fails to look at things that are always there. I don't mean that I avoid looking at them. It is just that these days I scarcely read books, so why would I look? I am not even sure why I keep them, except that I have owned many of them for a long time, decades in the case of some. They even smell old, like old clothes and old mattresses. I once read that for damaging a person's health old books are worse than cats. Books are, now that I think about it, among the few personal items that are impossible to wash. The rat is making a dreadful ruckus. It has its forepaws up against the glass again. It is chattering its teeth, producing an awful ratcheting sound, and its eyes are bulging; they look about to pop out of its head. If I felt more sympathy for it, I could imagine that it is trying to say something, puffing out its cheeks and spluttering in a futile effort to utter some matter terribly important to it, or else it is having a fit. I am going to have to change the chips at some point, and that will mean reaching my arm inside. I am not going to do that while it is in there. Maybe I can dump it in the bathtub while I do it. The last time I was still reading a lot was at Potopotawoc, where it seems to me I was reading almost all the time, mostly magazines, because I was not able to type much there, as I think I mentioned, and it was either read or fret, or look out the window at the falling leaves, or at the falling snow, and later, after a long time, at the new leaves, and so forth. *Only* magazines, as a matter of fact—I don't think I read a single book while I was there. I didn't own a television there, though up in the main building was a gigantic set that was always turned on even when no one was sitting around it, and sometimes I went up and watched. I don't have a television here either, having given the one I used to own to a young man who came to wash the windows ever-so-many years ago, as I might have mentioned also. I can already hear people saying, "What on earth did you do with your time, when you were not at work, if you didn't read or type and you didn't look at television?" The answer is that I really don't know. I took little walks, I cleaned the house a little, I prepared small meals, shopped for a few things, looked out the window for a few minutes, napped a little while, thought a little, and the day was gone—the littles and the smalls piled one on another and added up to all there was. It is not difficult to fill a day, not because I have so terribly much to do, but because time itself is moving so fast. The days, I want to say, wink past; even the tedious days are gone in a flash. I say that, and I have an image of the lighted windows of a speeding train. I have not been an active reader for some time now, but even after I stopped reading, except for magazines, I went on acquiring books, intending to read them at some point in the future, went on buying them even when I could not afford to. At various times in my life I have known people who, when they could not afford to buy books, would just steal them. Before he met me Clarence regularly stole books, though he would not steal anything else. In my experience people like Clarence usually think it is o.k. to steal books, where by "like Clarence," I mean aspiring writers. And I have known painters who regularly stole paints. Years ago, on a day like today, I might have gone out to a bookstore. I used to spend hours in bookstores, reading entire chapters while standing at the shelves, and occasionally people would come over and stand beside me and say things like, "I see you are reading X or Y. What do you think of it?" More pages have tumbled off the table, falling with a fluttering sound like the wings of several birds. A jacket is the only significant thing that I can remember stealing—significant in contrast to trivial items like ballpoint pens and paper clips, which I also occasionally took from work, though I doubt that anyone, had they seen me going off with those items, would have cared. I took the jacket last fall. A man tapped on the glass of the outer door while I was in the room sorting. Since Brodt was upstairs I opened it myself, and the man handed me a woman's leather jacket that he had picked up from the floor of the garage. I hung it over the back of my chair, meaning to give it to Brodt when he came back, but I took it home instead. I don't recall taking anything else, except, as I said, minor things like paper clips, and once a large blue stapler and another time a miniature radio no bigger than a cigarette pack. I left the earphones, because I thought I would not like having plastic buttons in my ears, but when I got home I discovered the radio could only be listened to in that manner, not having any speaker of its own, and I threw it away. I certainly was not taking things on a regular basis. Even so I think Brodt became suspicious at one point. One Friday, when I returned from distributing upstairs, my paycheck was lying on the table as always, and when I opened my handbag to slip it in I noticed the contents were not in the usual order, as if they had been rummaged with. Brodt could not have seen the man handing me the jacket, but he might, I thought, have bumped into him later, perhaps sat next to him at a ball game the following weekend, for example, where they could have fallen into conversation, the man happening to mention that he had dropped a leather jacket off at Brodt's office the other day, at which point Brodt could not help putting two and two together. Or something like that. The incident of someone rummaging in my purse took place a long time ago, and I might not be remembering the sequence right. Maybe the rummaging occurred before I took the jacket, not after, in which case he was rummaging for some other reason, if he was rummaging at all. Why would he rummage? I like the phrase "trick of memory" for things like that, as when people, when they fail to recollect something in the same way as you, will say "I think your memory is playing tricks on you, dear," with the implication that memory is mischievous or even malevolent. I once took a sleeper from Seville, in Spain, to Heidelberg, in Germany. The cessation of motion at each stop along the way would rouse me from sleep, and I would lift the window shade and peer out at the platform and try to discover where we were. The names of the stations were posted on signs that hung above the platform, but sometimes the car I was on did not stop at a spot from which I could see a sign, even when I pressed my cheek to the glass, and I was astonished, at one point in the middle of the night, when I did see a sign, to discover that we were in Switzerland. Who would have thought that a train from Seville, in Spain, to Heidelberg, in Germany, would be passing through Switzerland? Though I traveled all over Europe, or that part of Europe one was permitted to travel all over in those days, I was never in Switzerland again, so if I had not awoken at that moment on the train from Seville or if the train had not stopped at just that point along the platform, I might have passed my entire life without ever knowing that I had once visited Switzerland.

In America I traveled by car and airplane, and later, when we had become more or less impoverished, by bus occasionally. Sometimes I rode trains in America also, mostly between New York and Boston, and Clarence and I twice took a train all the way from New York to Los Angeles and back. I am referring to passenger trains, of course—Clarence was the only person I know who actually rode freight trains, though he did it in order to write something for a magazine, which is hardly the same as really doing it. Obviously, even if I had not woken up or had woken up and not been able to read the sign, I would still have passed through Switzerland once in my life. On the other hand, had I not woken up, etc., and the train had actually gone only through France, as one would think it should, that would not have made a difference in my life; I mean, there is really no difference between sleeping through Switzerland and sleeping through France. Which makes me wonder if the important thing is what actually happened in the past or only what we remember having happened. I suppose I might at this moment be altered in some very minute way by the knowledge I possess now that Switzerland was among the countries I visited. On the other hand, I probably would still be changed in just that minute way had the train in fact gone through France and I had merely imagined it stopping in Switzerland; imagined it, I mean, because I misread a sign in a French station or because

I did not wake up at all and merely dreamed we were in Switzerland. Of course, if the train had gone through Switzerland, as I believe it truly did, and had fallen off a mountain on the way, that would have been very different from sleeping through France.

It was not as bad as I imagined. The moment I lifted the top, he shot into the pipe and stayed there, though the stench was dreadful. I took everything out, shoveled it out with a kitchen spatula, ready to whack him if he reappeared, and I cleaned the bottom with Clorox, provoking a tiny sneeze from inside the tube, like someone ripping a postage stamp. I put the dirty chips in a plastic bag that I set outside on the fire escape. France, when I went back there with Clarence one winter, was the second extravagance we undertook with my money, while there was still a great deal of it. The first was a trip to Africa. Even now, after all these years, it feels odd to think that I once went on a safari in Africa, and not the sort of excursion they call a safari these days but a genuine hunting safari with the goal of shooting as many large animals as possible, though we never did shoot an elephant, which is of course the biggest animal, a buffalo being the biggest that we actually shot. I personally did not shoot it, Clarence did, while I was at the hotel with a stomach disorder. It was not a hotel in the usual sense, just a long shed with bunk beds and a pair of tin-roofed toilets outside, where, if I had to use one in the daytime, as I did frequently while my stomach was disordered, I nearly suffocated in the heat and stench. The feeling I still have of the safari being a truly odd event in my life is probably due to the fact that it was out of character for me, though it was not out of character for Clarence. The photograph that was in the frame I broke the glass out of is from that trip. I removed it from the frame in order to pry the broken pieces from the grooves, and I have taped it temporarily to the window, where I usually only put notes, because it is a kind of note, being up there to remind me to buy another piece of glass. It shows Clarence with two dead lions. He is standing over them, a boot on the rump of one of them, which I think must be the male—they were a male and a female lion. The photograph was not taken at the spot where we shot them. They are on the ground in the middle of our camp, the Africans having just dumped them there after dragging them from the back of the Land Rover, two men pulling on the legs until they fell out. You can see the rear part of the Land Rover in the background. The lions fell one on top of the other. Their heads are cut off in the picture is the reason I can't tell whether Clarence has his foot on the male or the female. In fact, so much of them has been cut off in the picture that if one did not already know they were lions one might think Clarence was standing next to a couple of sandbags, or bags of wheat or something, with his foot on one of them. He is standing with a glass of champagne in his raised hand, though naturally you can't tell just from the photo what he has in the glass either—it was champagne, though, from the last of a great many bottles we had bought in Nairobi for occasions of this sort, when we (that being Clarence, usually) shot something large. We had used up the last of our ice a few days prior, and the wine was warm and sickening, I thought, though I don't recall Clarence minding. I had been standing next to him a moment before, clinking my glass to his, and had stepped out of the frame to snap the photo. I was quite giddy from having shot a lion, which is probably the reason I left important things like their heads out of the picture. I regret shooting it now, though it was easy to do at the time, while I was still under Clarence's influence. It seems to me that I was quite happy then. I don't mean that I was happy then on the whole, just that I remember being happy for most of that particular trip, happy in a way that made it easy to be indifferent to the feelings of others, especially lions, who are themselves famously indifferent in that way. It was during this trip also that I took up Clarence's habit of whistling for the servants. When I say it was easy to shoot the lion, I mean, of course, that it was morally easy; it was in fact a rather difficult shot. And when I say that I was under Clarence's influence, I mean I was under his influence in regard to extraneous things like shooting lions and playing tennis, but when it came to most other things he was under my influence. Once years ago when Potts and I were still seeing if we could be more than just considerate neighbors, she was visiting up here and asked about that photograph, and I told her all about the time I had shot the lion. I think she was quite horrified when she realized how much I had enjoyed doing it. I am surprised that she has trusted me with her rat. Even with so much left out of it the photo is still quite true to life. I mean if one thinks about Clarence in later years one does tend to see a man standing alone with a drink in his hand, and if one really does mistake the lions for sand-bags, then it becomes truer still, capturing the aspect of being embattled that was characteristic of those years—embattled, but also fortified, the latter referring to whiskey, of course, but also to the feeling he got later from his prox-imity to Lily, it seems to me, the illusion of being fortified. He felt fortified by the furious energy she brought to bear on everything at a time when he was running out of fuel, really, and which seemed to make him feel alive again, though it made me feel exhausted, but especially by her youthful beauty, by the fact that she still had it. There was the sym-metry and the clarity of her features, which had nothing loose or accidental, but I believe that what really drew Clarence and made him feel fortified was the fact that she was at that point of life and vigor where it was difficult for the idea of death to find an attachment point on her. I say to myself, Enough about Lily, and mean to move on, but I am tripped, or tricked—or trapped, even—by a sudden ingress of unbidden memory. Nothing, I think, in my mind is my own. She is sitting at the window in the yellow-papered house, wavy black hair shadowing a portion of her face. I can see the blinding Southern afternoon through the string curtain she has made for my window. The heat has silenced even the insects, stifling them. She is talking to me, but I don't hear any words—in my memory, I mean, I don't hear any words. Lily had a habit of looking out the window while she talked, in a way that made you feel you were not with her, that you were somewhere off on the horizon, not stretched out on a broken-down sofa, which is where I actually was, and she had a way of talking about the future as if it were a proximate space that one had only to step over into, not a possibly unattainable time separated from us by a chasm of unpredictability. Listening to her I realized—meaning I had a sudden very clear thought, dazzling in its obviousness— that she and Clarence were just alike. I don't think I said in so many words *they belong to each other,* though that was the feeling of it, suddenly. I don't know why I always remember the black hair, since her hair was brown.

Day before yesterday, I think it was, the last time I fed the fish, I forgot to put the lid back on the aquarium, and the snails must have climbed out. The snails obviously climbed out; there are no snails in the tank. I looked for them on the floor, and in the flowerpots, thinking those would be the sort of thing they would hide in, being snails, even if they are not garden snails. I found a flashlight in a kitchen drawer, intending to shine under the furniture in case they had crawled there. The bulb glowed a faint yellow for several seconds and then went completely out. I have left the top off the aquarium in case they decide to climb back in, as they might want to do, being water snails. I will have to watch where I step, especially on the dark-patterned carpets on which a brown water snail will be practically invisible. I sat in Potts's husband's chair and watched the fish while they ate, the miniscule wafers of food drifting slowly downward as gently as snowflakes, the fish dashing this way and that catching them in their mouths—snowflakes falling, I want to say, through the green air of summer. One year Papa carried me outside during a snowstorm, held me in his arms, and we walked up and down the driveway in front of the house. Giant cotton-ball snowflakes drifted down, and I opened my mouth and caught them, and the air then was blue and black. After watching the fish a while I dozed off in Mr. Potts's rocker, and it was dark when I awoke. The stairwell light is out and climbing back up the stairs I had to feel my way along the wall with my hands. I was reminded of the cover picture on my copy of *Crime and Punishment*—Raskolnikov climbing a dark stairway in just that posture, on his way to kill a useless old woman. And now, I thought, I am the useless old woman, on my way to kill . . . *what?* Time, I suppose. I had settled back in my armchair, when I remembered that I had forgotten to water the plants, even though I had set out with precisely that in mind. I went to the window and looked out. It is raining again. The rat is whirring in its wheel. For hours at a time it does that now, even in the middle of the day. It seems to have become more active in recent days—an effect of the weather, I suppose, though maybe I am just noticing it more, because of the rain. Two days ago, when I was typing up the bit about the days passing like the windows of a speeding train and the subsequent bit about not knowing whether I was in Switzerland or France, it occurred to me that I did not at that moment know what day of the week it was, the name of the window, so to speak, that was currently flying past. That is, I did not know what day of the week it was while I was typing, not while I was on the train, though, of course, I don't know that either after all these years, though I must have known it at the time—one cannot travel about, catching trains and booking rooms and such, without knowing what day of the week it is. Since I didn't know what day of the week it was two days ago, I don't, as a consequence, know what day of the week it is now, when I am once again sitting at the machine. I have been having a hard time lately keeping my thoughts from getting in a jumble. The jumble seems to become worse the harder I struggle to get things straight, as happens to insects in spiderwebs, when their struggle only makes things more difficult for them. Once when I was looking at the mess in my room I told Clarence I couldn't live in a state of disarrangement anymore. He thought I had said derangement, and I found myself yelling, "I don't need a *doctor*, I need a *maid*." It was typical of Clarence to miss a distinction like that.

I can feel it almost physically in front of me—a vast intransigence against which I keep knocking my head. I can't describe it exactly; I have never been able to obtain a clear view of it. Whether that is because it is too close or too far away I can't decide. I only know that it impinges, that it is made of something extremely hard that will break my head if I don't watch out, if I go on banging against it, and that it bars my way. On rare occasions, though, when the sun is out, the windows are open, and the birds are cheeping, I don't feel it there and I become hopeful. I make a first cup of coffee and carry it to the little table, too excited to linger over breakfast. There will be time for that later, I think, but first. . . . And I pull up the chair and wind a fresh sheet of paper into the machine. Yet even as I am doing this I can feel my confidence ebbing, slipping away despite my (mental) attempts to hold on to it. This has been going on for a long time. And something is wrong with the begonias—they have dropped most of their leaves and there is a white moldy-looking fuzz on the stems.

I rode a train and two buses to get to Potopotawoc. I was on the second bus for hours, bouncing and swaying on a narrow, twisting, mountainous road overhung by tree branches on which the leaves were starting to turn. I was there before any of the others. I stood on the steps of the Shed and watched them arrive, spilling from the vans and buses in their funny hats. Some were dizzy from the gyrations of the road and staggered and blinked in the cool, bright September sun, others whistled and shouted or pumped a fist in the air as they climbed down from the vehicles, while the ones who had arrived before them clustered with the staff at the edge of the parking lot and clapped and waved. In former days Potopotawoc had been a summer camp for boys, and locally it was still called "the Camp." For the residents too it was just "the Camp" and they called each other camper: it was "Hi, camper," when you bumped into one of them on a path, and "Pass the ketchup, camper," in the cafeteria. Unlike an actual camp, though, the others—the workers, the people in authority, if one can call them that—were not considered counselors—they were staff. "Staff" was sometimes a collective term, as in "Staff is having a meeting up at the Shed," and sometimes not, as in "Watch out, Staff is standing beneath your window," in a case where, when you leaned out, there was just one person crouching there. Some of the residents were famous in small ways, well-known in certain circles, but they were not distinguished, the circles were not distinguished, and they, the people, had gone to pieces or otherwise declined, lost their talent or impetus or whatever, and a stay at Potopotawoc was supposed to help them get it back; set them back on their feet, was the phrase. Considering their condition, the atmosphere was relentlessly jolly, partly I suppose because so many of them were oblivious—deluded is what they were, and a tidy number were drunks. Deluded about themselves and their prospects, I mean, deluded about their talent, not deluded in the wider hallucinatory sense. The camp consisted, geographically speaking, of a hill and a lake. On top of the hill stood a glass-fronted building of intensely modern style, with exposed girders and out-slanting walls of rough-hewn sandstone, called the Shed, in reference to the long sloping roof, which descended so low at the entrance that taller men sometimes cracked their heads going in, cursing. Next to it was an older and smaller brick building with decorative cornices and tall windows with steel muntin bars like an old-fashioned textile mill, and they called that one the Factory. Most of the residents, along with a portion of the staff, had rooms in the Factory. The rest of us stayed in cottages scattered about in the woods. I don't know if it was by accident or design that nearly all the noisy hypersociable types had rooms in the Factory, where most of the incidents occurred, parties as well as fights, though usually not fistfights—word fights and water fights, toilet paper sometimes. They threw books sometimes. Most of the fights took place at their parties, I think. I never went to one of those, but I could hear them from my cabin. A wide meadow ran from the Shed down through the middle of the woods to the lake. There was a rotting boathouse at the edge of the lake and three or four battered canoes that were always drifting off and getting stuck in the reeds on the opposite side. The lake was too swarmed with weeds for swimming, and there were never any paddles. Most of the cabins were on the other side of the meadow from mine, so I did not often run across people if I stuck to the paths on my side.

The inhabitants of Potopotawoc, excluding Staff, were either permanent or provisional. I was provisional, permitted to hover at the margins and look on for three weeks in the fall, they said, and then they would see—see what kind of fit I was, is how they put it in their letter. That made me laugh when I read it, because of the word *fit*, which irritated Clarence, who had worked hard, filling out applications and drawing on the influence of friends, to get me in. It was because of the pages Clarence had sent them, which he had gathered up without telling me—more or less at random, I am sure, since even then I never numbered—that they took me. He told them they were the first pages of my novel, the first chapter of a novel called *Brunhilde's Balcony* that I had been working on for twenty years, though they actually were not the beginning of anything, just some things I had typed, Brunhilde being a person like me in most respects, like me as I was when I wrote them, not so much like me now that I have had time to think. The perms generally looked down on the temps, except for the women temps, whom they tried to take for themselves. There were fights over women, because there were not many of them, cliques were formed, and some people were not allowed to sit at certain tables in the cafeteria. It was as if people merely by setting foot on the soil became instantly infected with the spirit of boys past, a spirit corrupted by age and failure into a kind of juvenile levity that they hoped would appear devil-may-care, though anyone could see that it was just desperate. And the new-comers quickly succumbed: they might tumble out of the vans tight-lipped and hollow-eyed, but two or three days later, when I would bump into them at ping-pong or check-ers, they would be perky as titmice. "Hi, camper," they would chirp, "up for a game?" I had no idea why I was there. Staff organized them into teams; they played football and Frisbee in the meadow, and I heard them at night in the canoes, paddling about in the lake with their hands. Somehow or other I became mixed up with the perms. I don't mean that I associated with them in particular, in a convivial way, aside from checkers, but that the people in charge took me for one. I was there every day, looking more or less rooted, and after a while no one thought to say "What are you doing here?" Perms were not expected to leave, or they were not expected to leave permanently—they went away in the fall and reappeared in spring, like ducks. Most of them reappeared, I should say, along with others who had not been there before or had not been there for a long time. And in that way Potopotawoc was constantly renewed.

"Interesting," someone said, the constant advent of new people; "interesting and rejuvenating," that person said in a speech during the conclave in the Shed at the start of the second session. Looking around at the people, I could scarcely tell one from the other.

I stopped typing and went over and sat in the armchair. I was trying to remember, but the rat was scratching. Maybe it has fleas. When it scratches it thumps its elbow against the glass. I am not sure that part of a rat is an elbow. I was conscious of how much of Clarence has slipped away, but I could not think because of the thumping, and I said to myself, "Oh well, I will pick up my pages," indicating in my mind the pages that have slipped off the table, which is pretty much all of them now. They are scattered across the floor, as I am sure I mentioned, and I have been walking on them. I have almost slipped a few times, because they skid about when I step on them. I put a sofa cushion on the floor and knelt on that, and reaching out as far as I could I dragged the nearest pages to me. I tried using one of the broken fronds as a pull-stick to drag the more distant ones nearer, but that was too wobbly at first and then it snapped. I made a stack of all the pages I was able to reach. Nigel had stopped thumping. I glanced up, and he was watching me, whiskers twitching, I imagine, though I was not close enough to make out anything as small as whiskers. I crumpled up one of the pages. Looking down at the floor as if inspecting something there and mashing and kneading slowly, so as not to arouse suspicion, I squeezed the crumpled page into a tight little ball. I lifted my head: he was still looking. "*What are you staring at?*" I shouted, and I hurled the balled-up paper. I had the feeling while I was throwing it that it was going to crash right through the glass wall of Nigel's tank like a stone. It left my grip, flew a few feet, and dropped to the floor, arrested in midflight as if swatted down by an invisible hand. I crumpled another. I balled this one up even tighter by rolling it around on the floor under the heel of my hand, while Nigel, unconcerned, watched me from above. This one flew the distance and struck the glass with a feeble tap. He jumped back but didn't retreat into his tube. I didn't make another ball—I can't continue balling up pages and expect to make headway. I hoisted myself back into the armchair and sat there, clutching the chair arms, my heart pounding. I was glaring, or glowering, probably. Nigel was spinning in his wheel.

Today is Thursday. I went to Starbucks to find out what day of the week it is. At a table by the window was a woman I used to be friends with, but she seemed not to see me, and I am not going to talk about her now. And while I was there I ate an almond croissant and read the newspaper. I don't usually buy the newspaper—I take a copy from the rack, read it, and put it back—because I am not interested in much that is in the paper these days, except the crossword. I went to Starbucks instead of the diner, where I usually go for coffee, because the newspapers at the diner are inside a coin machine on the sidewalk in front. Before putting the newspaper back on the shelf, I tore out the crossword puzzle, holding the paper against my thigh under the table and tearing very slowly, to not make a ripping noise. Usually when I do that I also write in pencil above the headline of the paper, "No Crossword Puzzle in This Paper"—that way anyone who wants the crossword puzzle, who like me, perhaps, is buying the paper only for that reason, will know to choose a different copy. I didn't bother doing that today. I don't know why. On the way home I stopped at the grocery and bought batteries for the flashlight and seedless grapes in a transparent plastic bag. Instead of Elvie a young woman I don't know was at the register. Where in the world do grapes come from at this time of year? I wonder if I have mentioned the season. Probably not, but I am not going to look back through all my pages to check. Instead, I will say right now, for the record, that by "this time of year" I am referring to late spring. It cannot be winter, obviously, or I would have mentioned being cold, which I am sure I have not done since I talked about my trip to the typewriter store, a trip that, at the time I mentioned it, was already weeks in the past. We have not for months had the sort of unbearable cold we had during the pit of winter and that I would certainly have touched on had I been typing then. At times, when Clarence and I were relatively impoverished, the houses were so cold I wore fingerless gloves while I typed, and also later, during the winters at Potopotawoc. I never thought of wearing gloves like that when I was horribly cold in the farmhouse in France, which I intend to talk about at some point, and that is odd, since I recall that one of the workmen who came to replace windowpanes in Papa's house one snowy winter day was wearing gloves just like that, so I must already have known about them when I was in France, known that things like fingerless gloves exist. I bought my first pair at a hardware store in Ocean City, New Jersey, when we were impoverished near there. At Potopotawoc I came across a pair of wool gloves under a chair in the Shed and snipped the tips off the fingers, but even so my fingers turned blue on the really cold days. And that might be the reason I stopped typing there, and not anything that was going on in my head or anything people said. One day I forgot and wore those gloves when I went up to the Shed, and a camper said, "Hey, aren't those my gloves?" When he saw I had cut the fingers off, he said, "Hell, you might as well keep them now." I don't know if I have mentioned this before, the fact that I stopped typing there. That was the only time, before coming here, that I completely stopped typing for a long while, though Clarence had tried several times to convince me that I ought to stop, when he thought I was typing too much and not eating properly, by which he meant at a table in a civilized manner instead of at the machine, especially when we went on vacation. In fact I hated getting crumbs in the machine and never ate there unless I was typing things I was afraid of losing, worried they would fall out of my head if I went and sat at the table with the others, paying attention to their conversation and so forth. Clarence wanted me to pay attention to the country-side, which was green and peaceful, probably, or sun-struck and stark, depending—we went to a variety of places on vacation. In Starbucks there are always a lot of people typing on computers. I see their fingers moving but I don't hear any sounds, and I am not able to banish the suspicion that they are pretending. They did not, at Potopotawoc, want to give me back my typewriter at first, but I insisted. I told the director I was not going to leave his office until he gave it to me. And I kept it with me after that, carrying it up and down the hill between my cabin and the Shed several times a day and resting my feet on it in the cafeteria.

It was a Smith Corona in a hard plastic case with a handle that made it look like a small suitcase, so carrying it was not as difficult as one might think. But I was still worried that someone was going to take it while I slept. I had brought along a length of clothesline for stringing my wet clothes across the room as I did at home when we were relatively impoverished, and I used some of that to tie the typewriter to my wrist at night. It was heavy string, as I said, and not wire, so obviously anyone who wanted to could have cut it with scissors. My thought was that since they couldn't know the string was going to be there it would not occur to them to bring along scissors, and without scissors or a knife they would be flummoxed by the truly difficult knots I had learned to tie when I was mountain climbing with Clarence. After a while, though, when I realized that I was not going to be typing anyway, I stopped carrying the typewriter around, and I did not use the string anymore either. I was on my way home from there, I was sitting in Penn Station, and somebody actually did steal that typewriter, just reached over the back of the bench I was sitting on and took it while

I was trying to make sense of my ticket. I got off the train in Trenton and bought another just like it, even though I was not sure I wanted to type anymore.

It was dark when I went down to Potts's place. I stepped through the door and was reaching for the light switch, when I heard the crunch. I was wearing shoes. I don't know how many of them there were to start with—more than one, surely. I gathered it up with a Kleenex and put it down the toilet. Clarence loved raw oysters and laughed when I told him they were still alive when he swallowed them. I think I should get rid of my books. After all, I haven't read much in quite a long time, and I expect that I won't read at all in the future, now that I am typing again. I do, it is true, sometimes glance at the titles while going to and fro in the hall, if I happen to stop there for some reason, to steady myself by holding on to a shelf, for example, if I happen to become dizzy between the kitchen and the living room, or to recollect whatever it was I had been setting out to do, if I have lost track, and just a fleeting glimpse is enough to set me thinking, remembering what the book was about or what was happening in my life when I read it for the first time. I was reading *Winesburg, Ohio* for the first time when I met Clarence. It is not, in fact, entirely misleading to say, as I used to at parties, that *Winesburg, Ohio* caused us to meet— it was, at any rate, the excuse he found to stop and talk to me, since he had just been reading it himself. I was reading it on the steps of the Metropolitan Museum, because it was warm there in the April sun, sheltered from a cold wind blowing out of the park, and that was where he stopped to speak to me. He had come there to educate himself about art. That was his phrase: "I want to educate myself about art." And he *said* he had just been reading *Winesburg, Ohio*, is how I ought to have typed that, because when we began discussing the book he did not seem to remember it very well. In that way, in the way of being carriers of memory, books are like photographs. *Light in August* would be another good example: one glance at the yellow-and-black dust jacket, and I am back in the huge farmhouse in France where Clarence and I once spent an entire winter. That was his first time in Europe, but it was my third time as an adult. There was a tremendous cold spell in France that year, so cold that big chunks of ice were floating in the Seine—there were pictures of them in all the papers—and the cold forced us to retreat into the kitchen and keep a fire going in the fireplace day and night, eating and sleeping in that room, even though the house was enormous, with five or six bedrooms. The fireplace too was enormous, and the heat went right up the chimney—we had to sit practically inside it to feel any warmth at all—and my hands were so cold I could scarcely turn the pages of the book I was reading, which was *Light in August*, as I said. I had bought it at the little English bookstore on the Rue de Seine in Paris, thinking I ought to like it, because I had liked *The Sound and the Fury*, but it turned out not to be my sort of book at all. Even so, I have kept it all these years, packing and unpacking it I don't know how many times since then. Oddly, I have not experienced this as a burden until now. Not just *Light in August* feels burdensome now, but all my other books too. Or maybe it is not the books that are the burden but the memories; packing and unpacking them. While we were peripatetic, which was most of the time we were together, we lugged steamer trunks full of books around with us, along with Clarence's guns and golf clubs. We did not physically carry them along while we were traveling—that would have been too inconvenient— we had them shipped ahead to the place we were going. The only time we took all our possessions along with us was on our last trip, when we carried everything down South in a Pontiac station wagon. Nigel is in his wheel, making it whirl and whir. I scarcely notice anymore; and then I do notice, suddenly, and have to tap on the side of his tank to make him stop. Sometimes, when I do that, he jumps out of the wheel and then jumps right back in again.

We used to read to each other. Going to bookstores, talking about books, and reading to each other were the things we did most together in the beginning. We took turns reading chapters; and when there were long stretches of dialogue or when we read plays, we took turns with the voices. We read mostly in bed, but also, especially in our early period, we read facing each other in chairs or side by side on a sofa, on a bench in a park, on the train going west and back. I don't know why we stopped reading together, but gradually we were not doing it regularly, and then without realizing it was happening we were reading different books, and gradually we came not to care about the book the other one was read- ing, because it was not the book that we were reading, and we became bored and drifted off when the other one talked about his book. What we were doing, reading different books, was furnishing different rooms, constructing separate worlds almost, in which we could sit and be ourselves again. Of course those were rooms in which we each sat alone, and we gradually spent more and more time in them and less and less in the house we lived in together. When Clarence was gone I don't think I became more alone than when he was home at the end. If I were to open the door today and by some miracle discover him sitting on the landing, it would of course come as a surprise, since it would, given the circumstances, be a genuine miracle, but leaving that aspect aside, it would not make any difference—he would be sitting on the landing reading something I am not interested in, I imagine, so we would probably not try to talk about that. What would we talk about?

I really ought to give away the books I still have, if I am not going to read them. Though I would have to contend with the empty shelves then. Imagine becoming dizzy on your way down a hall and having nothing to hold on to but some bare shelves. It would be like fainting in the subway.

I must have been pretty once, what I call pretty. "Oh she was pretty once," I think they said, some people have said, seeing me now and thinking. The fact is I was never what most people would call classically pretty. I suppose I was homely. I had a domestic look, which infuriated me, because I knew that what was within did not correspond, as if I was prevented by my face from appearing as I was—I was coming out into the world, but my face stood in the way. Clarence stopped to talk to me, and it was not because I was especially pretty, I thought, but because he was able to see what was within. If this becomes a book I will want to put in a few words about my own appearance at that time. "Thin," "stoop-shouldered," "light-brown hair," "large chin," "hazel eyes," "flat chest," "intense, darting gaze" are some of the words I might put in, I suppose, if I put in any. I will also, in a book, want to describe myself at present more thoroughly than I have up to this point, and that will be difficult.

I have propped a small mirror against the coffee cup, so I can see myself while I type. I am now looking at myself closely: I see an eye. What is the eye like? It looks. I suppose it blinks, though I can't see it while it does that. When I was a child I tried to see myself with my eyes closed. I wanted to know if my shut lids were little wrinkled pleats like the lids of my two small cousins when we squeezed our eyes shut in games or if they were smooth and blue-pale like Mama's on hot afternoons when she was resting on a sofa. In the mirror I see a woman (is that important?) of indeterminate age, an older person; how old is unclear. Her hair is thin and apparently cut at home by its owner. A curved back (I can't see that in this mirror), a bump in the upper spine, not quite a hump, a significant bulge. She often wears earmuffs, even on warm days, because of the noise of the traffic and the compressors. She will be glad, she says, when she goes deaf.

Giamatti has telephoned again. I told him, soon. And I have posted a new note: Feed the Fish. I taped it where I can see it while I am typing, just above one I wrote years ago, in tiny letters in red marker on a lined index card that has now turned dun with age, the ink so faded I would not be able to make it out if I did not remember what it said: "Thunder suddenly sprang again outside with a clap and bang, slithering." I put it up there because it is one of the best short sentences I know. Maybe not one of the best I know period, but one of the best short ones I know about Mexico. I put new batteries in Potts's flashlight, and shining under the furniture I found the snails, all of them, I think, wedged in the crack between the wall and the plywood back of the cabinet the aquarium sits on, all the way down on top of the baseboard. They looked dried out. They had set out, I suppose, in search of greener pastures, thinking (sort of) there might be a nice weedy pond just over the horizon. It is interesting the way human folly extends all the way down through the animal kingdom to snails—they behaved, I want to say, just like Clarence. I tried to pull the cabinet away from the wall, to get at them with a broom handle, but it was too heavy, because of the weight of the aquarium, and the slot was too narrow for the broom handle, which got stuck when I forced it. Unable to pull it back out, I have left it there, the whiskery part of the broom sticking up and pressed flat against the wall back of the aquarium. I took a glass and scooped water out of the aquarium and poured it down on top of the snails. I don't know at what moment Clarence decided to become a writer. Not as early as I had, surely, since I was older and my background was more advanced than his. *Advanced* is probably not the exact word for what it was—rich in cultural opportunities is how a magazine might describe it. By the time we met I had been writing for many years already, while he had nearly finished pharmacy school before he finally decided. I say finally decided, because that is how he used to tell it, how he told it to me on the steps of the Metropolitan Museum the day we met. He always phrased it that way, despite the fact that, having finally decided, he did not then do anything to change the way he was living, did not let writing get in the way of his life, which was still quite ordinary and, to hear him describe it, industrious and humdrum. He did, I think, add a couple of English courses to his schedule at the university, and he tried to read books like *Ulysses* that people had told him were difficult and important, and he began to talk about himself in a new way, as a writer, which was foolish, since he had not written anything to speak of, but also important, because it set him up to do it, like a wager on his future. Clarence actually believed that he *ought* to read books like *Ulysses* and *Don Quixote* and *Tristram Shandy* even after I had explained how ridiculous that was if he didn't *feel* like reading them. He was sincere in believing things of that sort, and that he *ought*, as he said, to become informed about art, and his sincerity was what I found moving in those days. But he did not sit down and write yet, the moment he decided, because he was worried about money and wanted a way to make a living while he was getting established, "getting established" being another of his phrases. I have mentioned already how depressingly practical and calculating in a mercantile way he sometimes was, due to his background and his anxiety about becoming poor. When we met in New York he was living (I nearly wrote that he was *insisting* on living) in a parsimonious little one-room flat in the Bronx and working as a pharmacist at a drugstore in Yonkers, while trying to write short stories, where "trying" in those days meant sitting at a typewriter as I did and typing things one never finished.

I lay down, thinking I would rest a while. It was past four when I awoke, and for a few moments, before the room came into focus, I did not know where I was. I heard myself saying "hello, hello," the way I used to, when I would wake up late and wonder if anyone was home—anyone being Clarence, of course, except for a brief time after he took up with Lily, when anyone was Steven. Steven didn't last, and we never came close to the point where I would wake up and expect him to be there. I must have forgotten while I was napping that I live by myself now, and when I woke up and discovered it all over again, like a brand new fact, it came as a shock. The reason I almost wrote, a while ago, that Clarence *insisted* on living in that miserable place in the Bronx is that that was how it struck me at the time; I couldn't help suspecting that he was doing it on purpose, because up to that time I had not known any people, as friends, who were genuinely poor. I had known several people who were living actively in squalor, but they were doing it because they were bored with money, and poverty impressed them as chic and interesting, and all of them, except for two who died in an apartment fire, went back to being wealthy after a time. Clarence did not know anything when I met him, and that made him diffident. He was able to become enthusiastic about something only if he had permission, because he was afraid of making a mistake. He had joined a shabby little writers' group, and their opinions were all he had to go on, and since he was never quite sure what to admire, he admired what other people admired, and of course that was fatal. Sometimes, though, he was not diffident enough. He once carried on extravagantly about Modigliani in front of a group of my friends from that epoch, when we were first together as young writers in New York, before he had a clue, and one of the girls, whom I stopped speaking to afterwards because of it, egged him on to say guileless and ridiculous things. I happened to walk in on them, and he was talking about Modigliani and Lautréamont, though he did not know the first thing about Lautréamont. I strolled over and turned the radio up, to drown him out, but that caused him to talk louder, so I pulled him to his feet and made him dance with me. Later, though, he developed a whole set of opinions and stuck to them even after I had told him they were boorish and common. During our first year or so he was always excited about his writing, even though it was not any good yet, and by that time I was already tired; I was twenty-six and thoroughly tired. In college I had already become tired of the things that people group under youthful pursuits, despite not having actually pursued any of them except for a few weeks at the beginning of my first year, and now I was tired of adult things as well. It was partly because I was already tired, I think, that I was attracted to Clarence, drawn by the fact that he had no notion of fatigue of that sort. People said that I had allowed my life to be "subsumed" by Clarence (at least that is what I guess people were saying, what I suppose now they were saying then), when in fact the opposite was true: I possessed everything Clarence wanted, possessed, I mean, in my background and culture. I could divide the book into two parts: Edna Ascendant and Clarence Ascendant. Or I might call the second part Edna Descendant, that being more poignant and better capturing the feel of it, the way the slope downward felt to me, from my side, where it seemed ineluctable and inexplicable. A philodendron (I think it is) seems to be dead.

With the windows open wide I can hear the Connector clearly. It is louder on days like this one, with clouds, I have noticed, because the noise strikes the clouds and bounces back. Even though I know that to be true it still strikes me as strange—the idea of something invisible like sound bouncing off something soft like clouds. It is cooler today, but I am not closing the windows yet, because then I will have to look at how dirty they are, have to type in the dirty light coming through them. "An oldish woman is typing her life up in a room filled with dirty light" is how I might begin the book. I don't know why I am suddenly bothered by the windows, since they have been getting dirtier for a long time now, a little dirtier each day, I imagine, molecule by molecule, for years, plus the fact that I have covered so much of them with paper. Window washers are beyond my means. I am referring to the people, of course, not the instruments, which are really just a bucket, a squeegee, and a couple of rags, as far as I can tell. The instruments are not beyond my means, at least not in a pecuniary sense, though they are probably beyond my means at this moment, meaning this month, and the next one too, probably, unless something happens. But they are at any moment, meaning forever, beyond my means in the physical sense—I cannot imagine hanging out of a window in order to wash the exterior, where most of the dirt is, thirty feet above the sidewalk with my knees hooked over the sill. I expect the windows will go on getting dirtier, while the world, the building across the street, and the sun, become blurred, vague, and less cheerful. "Molecule by molecule her world grows dim" is how it will be, probably, and that might be the second sentence, by way of setting the stage for what is about to happen, or not. People will look up at my windows and see a shape moving on the other side of the glass, and they will not be able to tell if it is a man or a woman.

Clarence was quite good-looking in a rough way, a masculine way, it seemed to me even then, though the real masculinity did not come out until later, after he had put on flesh and grown a Clark Gable mustache. By the time he was thirty he was stocky and truly impressive in that masculine way. It was almost an Emiliano Zapata mustache at one point. When we met he was already masculine, of course, but in an ethereal direction, if that makes sense, slender and boyish, with startled eyes, so one did not see the tendency to become heavyset and brutal; and it was that startled quality, the feeling that he was seeing the world new, as if it had just come into being before his eyes, that drew me to him, because of the fatigue I mentioned, and it vanished completely in later years. The first thing he published—we had been together for three years already—was a short story, a memoir, really, about hunting squirrels when he was a boy, the minutiae of hunting them with a small rifle, and the importance of squirrels as food in those days, and in that way he brought in his childhood deprivation and suffering. He sent the typescript off to three or four literary magazines, which held onto it for months before turning it down without explanation. It was his good looks in that masculine way that finally got it published, in a national hunting magazine, because he went up to their offices in person after he had mailed it in to find out what they thought of it, and they took one look at him and what they saw made what he wrote seem authentic. It was an epoch when being authentic seemed important to people. It is interesting how things that seem obvious and are even part of the atmosphere of a certain epoch become incredible later—now, it seems, something or somebody can be blatantly fake and nobody cares. The deprivations of his childhood made what he wrote seem authentic and significant, but they also made him narrow-minded and intolerant of my life, because he thought that if one had not suffered in a crude and obvious and really external way, in the way he had suffered, and his family had suffered for generations, then one had not truly suffered at all and was just acting up or pretending. "Neurotic misery" was the phrase he liked using, to make it sound fake, and he thought, though he never dared say it, that if you had not suffered in that obvious external way, then what you wrote could not be authentic and significant either. That was a terrible mistake on his part and led him to include things in his stories—war, murder, rape, and the like, a great many adulteries and divorces, even the Jewish genocide once, and a famine in Africa, as a setting—that he regarded as significant events, in the belief that they would make the stories significant also, but of course all they did was make them ordinary. I told him it was not up to the events to make the story significant, but the other way around, but he was never able to see it that way. In the refrigerator this morning I found the grapes I bought some time ago, as I think I mentioned, and forgot about, wrinkled but intact otherwise, and I ate the whole bag while working on the crossword puzzle I took from Starbucks. I was not able to get all the answers. There was a time when I regularly got all the answers, but that has become impossible now that so many of the clues refer to television shows and celebrities one could become familiar with only by watching television—watching a large amount of television, it seems to me. In recent years even the puzzles in the *New York Times* have become like that and are now unworkable by people like me, literary people without television. Reflecting on it now, I suppose that is the reason I didn't bother writing my usual warning on the newspaper the other day, about the crossword puzzle having been torn out: because I don't feel a connection to the sort of people who are able to work the puzzles these days. I look at the puzzles, and at the people in the cafés with computers on the table in front of them, staring, and I think, Who are these people?

The grapes are not as delicious as I thought they would be when I saw them in the store, even allowing for their not being entirely fresh, having sat in my refrigerator for so long. They also have the wrong shape for grapes, being oblong like jelly beans, and their flesh is firmer than it ought to be, almost chewy. I imagine those are all signs that they have traveled a long way, which of course they must have done, since, as I mentioned, it is spring here, from Chile or even Australia, I suppose. Somewhere on the other side of the world people are picking grapes. In fact, machines are picking grapes there too, I suspect. The grapes were bred that way in order to travel this long distance intact, bred firm, for example, so as not to become crushed when stacked. When I was in France the first time as an adult, while I was still in college, when I went over there with Rosaline Schlossberg, I traveled down to a village near Avignon to pick grapes at the end of the summer—when I had been in Paris for only about two months, though I was expected home by then—with two German boys I had met a few days prior. I slept with one, and then with the other, and then with both. We slept in sleeping bags on the floor of a room above a stable. In the space below us they kept two oxen, and during the night we could hear them moving about in the stalls, and they smelled horrible at first, though after a few minutes with them one became so used to the odor it was impossible to smell it even if one tried. By "slept" I mean we made love and also went to sleep together, pressed to each other in the warmth of a sleeping bag. People are going to find my way of talking quaint, I imagine. Several of the foreigners I met in Paris were used to going down every fall for the vendange, because that was a way to earn a little money, which is what everyone said, but actually because it was a lark. When I say foreigners I am referring to people who were not French rather than to people who were not American, and it was a way for them to earn money because one did not need a work permit to pick grapes, and as for myself I picked grapes only that one time. One of the boys was named Karl; I have forgotten the name of the other one, though I do recall that he had a long chin and was not as attractive as Karl but was amusing in other ways. You don't actually pick grapes, you cut the stems using a knife with a curved blade, which if you are not accustomed to it, as I was not, quickly raises blisters on your hand. After work we went swimming in a little brook, and I sat on a rock in the middle of the stream and held my blistered hand under the cold water. I am going to want to leave this sort of thing out. It is amazing how much of one's memory consists of trifles.

I sprayed the fern again, making three times that I have sprayed it today, having forgotten yesterday and the day before, I forgot all last week, in fact. It seems overall less green than before, but perhaps that is an effect of light. I didn't forget every minute of the past week—sometimes I remembered and said to myself, "O.K., I am going to do that," and then I forgot. I have been careful not to spray close to the wall, and now the half of the fern on the wall side has turned brown. I am going to drag it out into the center of the room, so I can walk around it spraying. Clarence became concupiscent when he had drunk too much, randy in an ungainly and ruthless manner, especially in the middle years, when he was still quite good-looking in a heavy, knocked-about way, like a defeated prizefighter, and he regularly went off with young women he had met at parties or at readings, when he was still giving readings, or at sporting events, when he was writing about those for magazines. By "going off" I mean he would decamp with them from wherever they were at the time—the pool or party or whatever, stadium, tennis court—and also, metaphorically, that he would explode on meeting them, an appetite for some young woman or girl overtaking him in a rush, like a fit, really. It looked, I told him, practically pathological. But the fits, overwhelming while they lasted, would vanish as quickly as they came, in a twinkle: they would go poof and land Clarence on his bottom, collapsed in a chair or on the grass, red-faced and gasping, sprawled and beached, I could say, sometimes still wearing his cartridge vest, looking perfectly ridiculous. Ridiculous also because the targets of his infatuations were, until Lily, so unsuitable, as everyone but he could see from the outset—it took him a day or two longer, usually; it took him a month in one case. He had an especial weakness for college girls, his defenses, such as they were, being easily overpowered by the adoration of well-formed, sexually charged young women with undeveloped wiles and a smattering of education, girls or women who were simply not equipped to penetrate his charms. Whenever we visited a campus or went to a party with that sort of girl around I had to prepare myself for an explosion or escapade. I was not accorded a similar latitude, naturally. Not that I wanted it. Even in Venezuela, it was just a matter of dropping in on a few nightspots with some of the crew while he was working, and even that was too much for him. I don't think he cared in a personal way what I did by that time; he was worried that I would make him look bad in public, especially in Venezuela, where men are so cruel. When he passed through the hotel lobby, where a lot of them would be lounging about, drinking Scotch and talking loudly, one or another of them was sure to hold two fingers to his head in imitation of horns. And Clarence did not make it easier for himself by wearing the straw hat, as if he were hiding something. They wiggled their fingers behind their heads, which of course horns do not do—horns, I mean, don't wiggle. I told Clarence they looked as if they were pretending to be rabbits. He did not find it amusing, though, and avoided the lobby, going in and out of the hotel through the kitchen. After a while we gave up speaking about those things; not a single word, ever. What could we have said that would not have been unbearable? If Clarence and I had looked at each other once during the latter part of those years, which I don't think we ever really did, we would have seen just ravages. The fact is, Clarence was a child of the world, while I belonged in a nunnery.

After a long while, sitting there thinking these things, plus a lot of other things too trifling or fugitive even to mention, I put on my robe and went down to Potts's place. I switched on the light over the aquarium and sat in Arthur's chair and watched the fish. Now and then one of them would swim over to the chain of bubbles rising from the air pump and drink a bubble, like a person swerving aside to sip from a drinking fountain—if fish could talk they would call breathing drinking, probably—and I thought of Lawrence's poem about fish. Loveless and never touching. No fingers, no hands and feet, no lips. Sometimes a fish swam over and looked out through the glass. I suppose it could see me sitting there in Arthur's chair, as if in a tank of my own looking out at it, it might have been thinking. Back upstairs, after switching off the lights, I went over and stood at the window awhile and looked out at the street. It was late and there was no one down there. I was turning away when I caught sight of what I thought was a large rat on the pavement across the street. I turned back just as it was creeping under a parked car, and I remained at the window, watching, until it emerged on the other side: a small half-starved cat, a broken hind leg causing it to creep like that. I tapped on the pane in an attempt to make it look up. Had it remained under the car, I suppose I would remember that one night while looking down from my window I had seen a large rat. I had left the radio on when I went down to Potts's place and now, as I was preparing to switch it off, I happened to notice they were playing Saint-Saëns's *Carnival of Animals*. I am not a highly sexed person. I don't know if that is evident to outsiders. I mean, how could someone tell, seeing me and Lily together, that one of us was highly sexed and the other not? Apart from the difference in our ages, one naturally assuming the younger will be more highly sexed. On the other hand, the older one, just because she is older and not as attractive as the younger, might feel sexually deprived and even desperate, which is also something an outsider might sense. I am talking nonsense, of course—people obviously do sense it. Even when I was young they could tell that I was not as highly sexed as the others just by looking at me, as I could tell by the way they looked at me, or failed to look at me. I am not sure that Clarence cared one way or the other. That I was not highly sexed must have made him feel secure, since I was not always out there for grabs the way some women are, the way they cannot help being, because of the sexual charge that comes off them.

Something smells bad in Potts's apartment: an acrid musty odor, the smell, I want to say, of wet plaster and mushrooms, though neither of those is likely to be present, except maybe in the bathroom in the case of wet plaster—not in the bathroom lately either, since I have been forgetting to water there. I notice it the moment I step through the door. It seems to be getting stronger by the day. It might, I suppose, be the odor of dead snails and algae, those being the only things I can think of that were not in Potts's place until recently. I have walked all around the apartment two or three times trying to sniff out the source, but I can't discern where the odor is coming from. After being down there for a minute or two I am not able to smell it anymore, is the problem, like the oxen in France, their stench nearly knocking us off our feet when we stepped through the door after work but vanishing completely by the time we went to bed, or the roar of the compressors on the roof of the ice cream factory, which I have to strain to hear. I have to strain to pay attention, and then I hear. All our senses are like that, more or less. I am sure I don't notice ninety percent of the things around me ninety percent of the time. I don't even notice that I am not noticing anymore, unless I pause and truly think about it as I am doing now. "Edna gradually failed to notice that a film of insignificance and tedium had coated the things of the world" is how I might describe it. I want to say that this dullness, this incapacity to notice, is merely a natural product of familiarity and habit, but I fear it might actually be produced by a weariness with looking. "She has looked at the world a long time, and has grown tired of it." Which might be why the notes I tape to the windows seldom have their intended effect. I stick them up there in order to have them where I can't possibly miss them if I open my eyes at all—I have only to turn my head in the general direction of the windows and they are right there in front of me. Yet after just a few days I don't see them anymore—I *can't* see them, is my point. Now that I am actively looking I notice a Post-it on the window to my left, above Clean the Bathroom. This one is in red marker and reads: Return Library Books. I have no idea how long that note has been up there. I don't know what books it refers to. The note, in fact, is thoroughly opaque, as I have not visited a library in years. After turning off the lights in the living room, I went over and stood at the window as I do nearly every night. It was late and the street was deserted. On the opposite sidewalk, illuminated by the lights of the factory, a woman was walking in the direction of the Connector, in housecoat and slippers, her arms around a plastic bag so full she had to tilt her head to one side to see where she was going. Viewed from above she looked like an ant carrying an enormous crumb. A police car rolled by, slowing as it came abreast of the woman, who did not turn to look—slowing menacingly, it must have felt to her—and then went on. She was almost at the corner when the bus came. She lifted an arm, but she was not at a regular stop, and the bus rolled on past her. From my window I could see into the lighted interior, the driver's blue-jacketed shoulder, his arm and a portion of the steering wheel, a line of empty plastic benches.

Sometimes a blank space lasts for days. I sat at the typewriter, but I didn't touch the keys. I sat at the table where the typewriter is, not *at* the typewriter precisely, just staring at the windows, though not in fact seeing them. Not typing, not seeing, not thinking really, or if thinking not remembering what I thought. I wrote a postcard to Grossman, in pencil, telling her that I had changed my mind, that I would be happy to write a short preface. The card sat on the table for a day or two, and then I threw it out. I went to the park every day except the day it rained. I went over there yesterday afternoon with a bag of crumbs—the pigeons in the park will eat out of your hand if you are patient. All the benches were occupied, and I don't enjoy sharing a bench with strangers, so I dumped the crumbs in a heap next to the trash can and started back. I was approaching my building on the opposite side of the street, when I noticed a man standing in the middle of the sidewalk, hands in pockets, looking up at my windows. He was wearing a dark waist-length jacket, perhaps a leather jacket, and a red baseball cap pushed back on his head. As a rule I don't pay attention to people I encounter on the sidewalk, my gaze being more or less directed to the ground in front of me, more or less focused. If I see feet on the pavement in front of me, I veer to one side or the other. So it was sheer chance that I happened to glance up and notice the man. I stopped and looked more intently, in part because he was staring up at my building, but mainly, I think, because he looked like Brodt. I am not sure it was Brodt, it might have been someone else with a profile resembling his from a distance—a great many over-weight men of a certain age, seen from a distance, have profiles like that. But in the confusion of the moment I failed to reflect on that fact and just assumed it was Brodt. I didn't *assume* it either, actually, in the sense of making an educated guess after weighing the evidence. "I looked up, and there on the sidewalk ahead of me stood Brodt" was how it was exactly. I was surprised, of course, and my thoughts leaped to the various things I had removed from work—stapler, jacket, and other items I mentioned, I think, scissors, paper clips, and so forth—and I stepped off the sidewalk into the street behind a parked van. If he turned in my direction, I did not want to be conspicuously there, stock-still and staring. I could see him through the windows of the van, though, and he seemed disinclined to turn, planted as he was with eyes nailed to my windows. It was afternoon rush hour, and he had placed himself squarely in the center of the busy sidewalk. Some passersby veered around him, creating a little eddy where he stood, while others, seeing him looking up at my building, slowed their pace and looked up also, expanding the eddy, though none of them stopped. After a few minutes he seemed to shrug. He crossed the street to a brown sedan parked almost in front of my building and drove away. I say *seemed* to shrug, because I was not close enough to see anything as small as a shrug. I have put the shrug in in order to lend an air of discouragement to his actions, though the discouragement too is just an assumption on my part: I was thinking that he had probably tried the doorbell and after getting no answer had walked across the street to see if he could tell from my windows if I was home, and then, not learning anything from that either and feeling discouraged, he shrugged, probably. Of course he could not have learned anything just by staring up at my windows unless I had happened to be standing there when he glanced up, which I actually might have been doing had I been at home, since I might have walked over to the window to see who was down there pushing the buzzer. On the other hand, it is also possible, as I suggested, that the person on the sidewalk was not Brodt at all but someone else of roughly similar profile, and furthermore, even if this person, whoever he was, had in fact been pushing a buzzer in my building, it was more likely to have been Potts's buzzer, in which case it was her windows he was staring up at. Or perhaps he had not buzzed at all. He might have been someone hired by the landlord to make repairs to the building, in which case he was probably not staring so much as studying, estimating materials, and so forth, in which case it is unlikely that he shrugged. I lay awake a long time last night, making a mental list of the items I had taken from work and wondering which ones Brodt was on to, if it was Brodt, as I was convinced in the delirium of half-sleep it must have been. The list was not huge, and I am not entirely certain that I had taken all the items on it. I might have merely considered taking some of them, picking them up perhaps, or shifting them around on a shelf, thinking that I could. I will have to go through my closets and drawers to make sure, even though failure to discover an item there won't prove anything: sometimes after leaving work with an item in my handbag I would realize that I had no use for such a thing and throw it out on my way home or leave it on the bus seat. I distinctly recall doing that on several occasions. But even as regards the items that I am sure I did take—trivial doodads like paper clips and ballpoint pens, as I mentioned, and a small porcelain frog, a hairbrush, and a few other things—I cannot see why after all this time they would want to send someone to spy on me. Unless, of course, they have decided to make an example of me, and why would they want to do that? It is possible, I suppose, that Brodt knew all along that I was taking things—after all, he had cameras watching me everywhere I went except in the women's toilet, and I don't recall taking anything from the women's toilet except a roll of paper now and then. In that respect the building might as well have been made of glass, not just on the outside, which it actually was—blue glass in which on nice days one could watch the clouds sailing—but on the inside as well. He could see me even in the elevators, even when I wedged myself into a corner, due to the convex shape of his lens. I always took an elevator when I had the mail cart, not being able to drag the cart up the stairs, though it was all the same to Brodt, I am sure—his eyes were everywhere, in halls, offices, stairwells. I tried not to look at the cameras, but sometimes I couldn't stop myself and would steal a glance, even though I knew he would see me doing it. Those would have been the only times our eyes truly met—his met mine, that is, not mine his, unless one considers the lens of the camera to be his eye, which I could not help doing.

Looking in both closets and in all the drawers in the bedroom and kitchen, I found the stapler, two pairs of earrings, sunglasses, the little porcelain frog, a topaz bracelet, a hairbrush, a wool scarf, a pair of leather gloves, and a small silver pocketknife. In the bottom drawer of my dresser I discovered a ream of typing paper that I took from work a long time ago, when I was still imagining that I might start typing again, and then forgot about, but I didn't add that to the pile. The jacket was hanging in the bedroom closet, and I put it with the rest. I stuffed everything in a plastic trash bag and tied the bag shut, and then I carried the bag down to the street and walked two blocks south and one east to where

DeLugia Construction Inc., says the sign, is working on a building that many years ago housed a bakery where I used to buy a warm breakfast roll every morning on my way to the bus, when I worked in the grocery store. By then it was well past midnight, and there was no one else in the street. They have placed a large dumpster against the curb in front of the building, where cars would be parked otherwise, and the building itself is walled off from the sidewalk by a tall plywood fence with yellow warning signs on it. The sidewalk narrows to a dark canyon where it passes between the fence and the dumpster, and midway through that I reached up and tipped the bag in. The dumpster must have been empty, the bag sending back a sharp metallic thud when it struck the bottom. A split-second after, as if in response, a sudden brilliant flashbulb-white effulgence lit up the horizon east of the Connector. Dumpster, street signs, the buildings across the street leaped into lurid view, then instantly collapsed into blackness, followed a moment later by a massive concussive boom. I felt something like a gust of wind against my body, but there was no wind. The windows in the building behind me rattled. I looked up and saw that a large sheet of clear plastic hanging from the scaffolding at the top of the building had billowed inward. I watched it settle back, rustling faintly. Walking back to my place I noticed a handful of lighted windows, but most of the buildings remained dark, and I did not turn on the lights in my place but went straight to the window and looked out across the roof of the ice cream factory in the direction of the flash. Except for the usual glow from the sodium lights on the Connector, nothing was there. And then I heard the first sirens, warbling and wailing, from several directions, joined by the impatient honking of fire engines. I glimpsed an ambulance, and later a police car and another ambulance, sirens wailing hysterically, going extremely fast across an intersection just three blocks to the south, but none came down my street, and they have all stopped now. Two men were shouting in the street, but they have stopped also. I listen, and all I hear now is typing—the sound of someone typing "the sound of someone typing."

Nothing yesterday. I slept until noon. I woke up late again this morning and was heating water for coffee when I remembered I had forgotten to buy milk on my way back from the park, forgotten because of the man standing on the sidewalk, I thought. The rat was moving about. Its food tray was empty. I pushed some pellets through the wire and refilled the water bottle, which was empty as well, and it rushed over and began to drink frantically, clutching the metal tube in its forepaws. I went around to the diner for breakfast. Walking by the ice cream factory, along the chain-link fence that closes off the parking lot, I passed a group of workers standing on the other side in unzipped snowsuits, smoking, and I smelled the smoke from their cigarettes. I sat in a booth next to the window. I had coffee, a fried egg, and toast. The diner was nearly empty, so I stayed on, watching people going by on the other side of the glass. I thought of the rat looking out through the glass of its tank, the fish looking out through theirs. I thought of eyes, the vitreous humor, the mind looking out through that. I drank four cups of coffee. The waitress told me her husband had won two hundred dollars in the lottery. She did not charge for refills. I was still there when a man at the counter got up and went outside and bought a newspaper. He came back in, walking and reading, and spread the paper open on the counter. The waitress scolded him for putting it on top of his plate. She pulled the plate out and held the paper up with one hand while she wiped beneath it. She put the paper back down, and the man and the waitress and another man stood looking down at it, resting the flats of their hands on the counter, the waitress, who was on the other side of the counter, twisting her head to see the paper right side up, and they talked about the explosion. An accidental gas explosion, just two blocks on the other side of the Connector, has blown a house to pieces, "blew it all to shit" the waitress marveled, exclaiming down at the paper. One of the men, a large man whose white shirt cradled rolls of fat slung from his waist, settled back on a stool. Standing at the register to pay I looked over the mound of his shoulder at the photograph: a rectangular hole surrounded by rubble, a wide scattering of shattered boards, a jagged hunk of mortared brick (most of a chimney, it looked like) on the roof of a small car, crushing it flat. Firemen in long black coats stood around in clusters, while more firemen and other people not in fire dress were climbing on the wreckage. Back on the sidewalk I fed my breakfast change to the paper rack and got my own copy, which now lies, picture up, on the table next to me. "The explosion," it says, "caused significant damage to adjacent houses, the shock waves knocking the windows out of several buildings on the block." Of course they mean knocking the windows *in*, the glass would have flown inward when the windows exploded—imploded, in fact—the shock waves coming from outside, obviously. A woman living across the street claimed to have been tossed from her bed by the blast, but I don't find that plausible. She thought the world was ending. Her husband rushed to the window (shattered) while debris was still "falling like hail" on the roof, and he thought an airplane had crashed. Only one person lived in the house according to neighbors, a man named Henry Poole, whose whereabouts are "unknown at present." I have a clear mental picture of a manila tag dangling from a pale-green IBM Selectric typewriter, one that I couldn't imagine carrying up my stairs, and I can see the penciled name: the initial *H* leans like a broken goalpost, the joined *o*'s look like lenses in a pair of spectacles. In a book with chapters, I might call this one "A Shocking Coincidence."

Using the handle of a broom I prodded the phone book out from under the sofa. I keep it there because it tends to flop over and fall out of the bookcase. I swatted the dust off with my hand. I sat in the armchair, the book in my lap, and went down the list of Pooles. There are more of them than I would have thought, having never met a Poole personally and not considering it to be a common name at all. The print in phone books is extremely small, and my crossword glasses were in the kitchen, so I thought I would just use a pencil to tick off the names, so as not to skip any. I had ticked off three or four when I noticed the pencil quivering. It was jerking, actually, a minute convulsion at the point that was quite obvious at the eraser end, due to the multiplier effect of the pencil shaft—it was an almost-new full-length pencil—a predictable perturbation, I suppose, considering the coffee. To still the tremors I gripped the pencil tighter and made it hop like a tiny pogo stick. Irritated, I clasped it in my fist instead, like an infant holding a spoon, and continued ticking off names, and at the seventh or eighth tick jabbed a hole in the page, ripping the forename off one of the Pooles. At that point I was extremely bothered, to use a phrase Mama liked. "I am extremely bothered," she would say, violently ripping pages out of a magazine. Ripping things—magazines, clothes, Papa's newspaper when she thought he was not listening to her, foliage she tore off plants and shredded—was one of the ways Mama expressed herself, expressed frustration, people would say today, though I find it difficult to think of her as frustrated, since nothing stood in her way. Like mother like daughter, I suppose. I tore the page out of the phone book, intending to carry it over to the window where I could see better. Nigel had come out of his tube and was standing with his front paws up against the glass, head cocked, watching me. "*What?*" I shouted, "*What?*" And before I knew it, even though I had decided I was not going to do that again, I had balled up the page and hurled it at him. It landed gently on the wire lid. I did not actually shout this time, I am almost sure I did not shout. It was more that when I looked at him I felt my thoughts shouting. I felt, I want to say, that they were about to explode. I have no idea what an exploding thought would be like. A scream, possibly. "Little Edna filled the house with exploding thoughts." And in fact that was exactly how it used to feel, now that I have said it. I sat there, bolt upright, or as upright as one can possibly sit in a chair of that sort— it is, as I think I mentioned, the overstuffed sort of chair one naturally sinks deep into—and stared at the tank. I think my eyeballs were popping out the way Nigel's sometimes do, but I was not chattering my teeth. They were clenched tight, I imagine. Nigel had retreated into his tube. I got up and went over to the sofa and shoved everything off onto the floor, making a great clatter and breaking the glass of another picture frame, and lay down. After a while it passed, whatever it was—being extremely bothered—passed. Looking up, I noticed cobwebs on the ceiling. Odd that I hadn't noticed them before, thick dust-clustered strands moving faintly. I sat up. Nigel was spinning his wheel again. I retrieved the balled-up page of the phone book. I got my glasses from the kitchen table. I uncrumpled the page and smoothed it against the tabletop. There is only one Henry Poole, on a street just over the Connector. I was already thinking of him as *the* Henry Poole.

It strikes me as odd that I find this interesting. I feel a personal connection, I suppose, is the reason: I saw his typewriter, and then weeks later I heard his explosion. And of course I did not just *see* his typewriter—I contemplated it from several angles, as I recall. Contemplated it mentally, that is—I saw it, physically speaking, only from the front.

He is (or was, possibly) a fellow typist. Henry Poole and his typewriter have impinged on my thoughts (invaded, actually) as something weirdly unusual. The coincidence impresses me as deeply, deeply meaningful, though I cannot for the life of me imagine what the meaning might be. I cannot, of course, entirely rule out the possible existence of other Henry Pooles, ones not listed in the phone book, though I think there are not likely to be many of those—not listed, perhaps, because he is impoverished and cannot afford a telephone or has a phone but under his wife's name or is disabled in some way and his wife or maybe his mother takes care of him, bringing him food and paying the phone bill, while he lies in bed and types. An IBM Selectric is a big machine to use in bed, though one could manage it, I suppose, by means of a large bed tray with feet, if the weight of it didn't drive the feet into the mattress. One would need a very firm mattress if one wanted to do that. This is not helpful.

The cafeteria at Potopotawoc closed at the end of September, stayed closed the whole winter, and I cooked for myself in my cabin. It was not a cabin in the sense of something pleasant and rustic; it was a hovel, actually—the roof leaked, I had to place cans and buckets on the floor, and sometimes I banged into them in the dark. On damp days in summer large snails crawled out of the woods and climbed up the walls inside, leaving behind them a film that glistened eerily in the lamplight. Sometimes I heard crunching on the porch at night and in the morning found little piles of crushed shell—the crunching was the raccoons eating them.

The few perms who stayed the winter assumed I was con-
nected to staff, and staff, I suppose, took me for a special
guest. No one ever asked me what I was doing there. I sometimes walked up to the Shed to play checkers. There was
almost always someone there to play with me. If it snowed
I did not go out, but on sunny days I sometimes walked the
whole way to the village. There was a filling station on the
outskirts that was also a grocery store and a flag stop for the
Greyhound, and I went there for groceries in winter and for
ice cream in summer. The Greyhound came by every afternoon, tearing past me on the road to the village, trailing a
gale of dust and gravel, and sometimes I thought of leaving
on it—no one would have stopped me had I done that, I
believe. I wore earmuffs the first winter there, because of the
cold, and again the next summer to shut out the chatter in the
cafeteria. I put them on too when staff organized games in
the meadow, touch football, as I mentioned, and Frisbee, to
shut out the shouting, cheers, and arguing, inevitably—staff
had always to be on the lookout for arguments and fistfights.
I was sometimes afraid, walking to the village, that I would
be attacked, as that had happened before, people said,
because of the homosexuals at Potopotawoc. No one seemed
to know for sure whether someone had actually been
lynched or only been threatened with lynching. I am not
homosexual, but I was not sure they would know this.
Nothing ever happened, and after a while I stopped feeling
frightened walking to the village. The rat is thumping again.
If it isn't thumping, it is whirring. In the middle of the afternoon. You would think it would get its fill of that during the

night. Unless it is sleeping at night and staying awake in the day just to annoy me. I am not going to stand for it much longer.

I bought a newspaper at the grocery and walked to the park. An elderly man followed me into the park and sat down on a bench opposite mine. He took seeds from a tin box on his lap and sprinkled them on the seat beside him and on the ground at his feet. He was wearing brown work shoes speckled with blue and yellow paint, and no socks. His ankles were thin and varicosed. The writing on the box was in French: it said *Crêpes à Dentelles*. I wondered if he was an artist of some sort, prompted by the paint speckles, the writing in French, I suppose, and his indifference to socks, but he was probably just painting his room. I had several painter friends in New York, and they all wore white tennis shoes without socks. In summer of course; in winter they dressed like everyone else. They have found Henry Poole lying face-down on the floor of the basement a few feet from an open gas valve. He died of asphyxiation, was already dead when the house exploded. Dead by his own hand, they are saying, though they have not found a note. "The blast took pretty much everything with it, including anything Mr. Poole might have confided to paper," they said. I like that phrase: confided to paper. Henry Poole, 52, a native of Tulsa, Oklahoma, repaired televisions for a living. A longtime Northside resident, he was, the paper said, "a familiar figure in the neighborhood, yet nearly a stranger to the folks next door." People reported seeing him walking a little brown dog at all hours of the night. A neighbor described him as "standoffish and kind of weird." The dog was discovered unscathed three blocks away in what the Humane Society calls a true miracle. I glanced up from the article to watch the pigeons arriving, crowding and bobbing around the paint-splattered shoes of the man on the bench, who was tossing handfuls of seeds. Poole had let his mail pile up on his front porch for the past several months; people saw him kicking it aside on his way in and out. This, according to the paper, was "a telling sign." What other kinds of signs are there? One night a windstorm blew a lot of the mail into the yard next door, and Poole went over in the morning, gathered it all up in his arms, and dumped it back on the porch. From there it continued blowing around the neighborhood in the days that followed, until finally one of the neighbors went up on the porch and stuffed it all in plastic bags. Tiny bits of debris, flakes of what some who touched them think was kapok from the upholstery, along with bits of paper and fiberglass insulation, "like pink snow," someone said, continued falling on the neighborhood for several hours after the explosion. I folded the paper and got up to leave. The man looked up at me, smiling. I was opening my mouth to say something pertaining to the birds, when they rose all together and he disappeared in a blizzard of clattering wings. I had been about to say, "I always forget to bring breadcrumbs when I come here," but I said "Good evening" instead. If this becomes a book I will want to take extraneous things out. Ditto for trivial remarks and pointless asides. Had he left a note it would have been typed on the IBM

Selectric I saw in the shop. More pages on the floor. The photo of Clarence and the lions that I taped to the window has come unstuck as well. I watched it flutter down, and my typing did not falter.

I sat in the armchair after supper and watched the light die. Then, later, I sat there again, in the dark, listening to the fading street sounds. I was thinking about how much I have forgotten, how little, out of the enormous scrap-and-litter heap that we call the past, I have managed to carry with me, how few of all the things and people I have known I still remember, how many have left no trace. Of course I can't actually *think* about things and people that have left no trace. I can *say* I am thinking about them, but I am really only thinking about the words "people and things I have forgotten." The words are there, like placeholders for things and people who have vanished, empty chairs reserved for those who are never going to sit in them again. Sometimes a thing or a person has a name still, but that is all, like a picture of someone that has been rubbed out except for their hat. The hat is there on top of the smudge—the hat is like the name of a person that time has rubbed out; or it is a hat floating down a river, when the person it belonged to has sunk and drowned, the river standing for the flow of time, obviously, and the hat standing for our words, bits of floating trash, anchored to nothing. I cannot think about a lot of Clarence, about, probably, most of the aspects of Clarence. No matter how often I say the name "Clarence" or use phrases like "Clarence was buttoning his denim shirt" or "Clarence had his foot on a lion," he does not approach; the words don't bring him closer; they just shovel him further under, bury him beneath a pile of empty chairs. And then I reflected on how easy it is to say things that are not true. For example, thinking about it again, I see that the story I told about the gardener was not entirely true, even though I believed it to be true while I was typing it. He did not actually put the mole in his pocket, as I maintained before; he dropped it down the front of his trousers. He was wearing wide blue suspenders, and he pulled the trousers out at the waist and dropped the mole in. Pulling the trousers out like that made an opening like a pocket, which must be the reason I said pocket before. I said pocket before because that was how I remembered it before, which does not help, that I actually remembered it wrong does not help, and now I remember it a different way. You cannot *remember* something one way and then *remember* it another way, different from the first way. You were not, obviously, actually remembering one of those times, maybe both. Clarence used to ask me, in regard to a passage in some piece he was writing, "Is this believable?" He wanted to make the things he imagined seem as real and solid as the floor he was standing on, he used to say. Real for him meant appearing the way we think they are. Everything not strange is invisible. In Avignon with the German boys, we could not smell the oxen. Sitting here now, I cannot smell Nigel, though I am convinced that the odor would knock me off my feet were I to walk through the door for the first time. My comfortable brown armchair over there is as distant as the moon, as distant as Avignon even. It is not that I don't always notice it: I can never do *more* than notice it—I cannot actually *see* it. Even when I make the effort I only manage to stare at it dumbly. What would it take to make it visible again? The same is true of names, I suppose. The word *chair* is as mute and dead as the chair itself. I wonder which died first. I think they must have perished together, in each other's arms, stifled by indifference and habit, wrapped in plastic film. If I had shown Clarence some of my typing in those days and asked "Is this visible?" what would he have thought? If I were to turn and see my armchair, suddenly, it would seem as strange and startling as a charging rhino, probably, or whatever it was that charged Clarence once, a hippo maybe. "Edna was struck dumb by a charging armchair" is how it would be. Mentally struck, that is.

I had a great many mice at Potopotawoc, and one day walking to the village I found a hungry cat and took it home. It was just skin and bones, and it ate all the mice, among other things—leftovers I saved from the cafeteria—and grew exceedingly fat. Other cabins had mice as well, and they put poison out for theirs, and my cat, having eaten all my mice, started visiting the other cabins in order to eat their mice, some of which were infected with poison. One day it came home ill, vomiting bile, crawled into my closet, and died. The director came down. He agreed that the cat had died from eating poison mice; it was karma, he said. I told him that was not my understanding of karma, that it would be karma only if he, the director, had died from eating mice, since he and not the cat had put out the poison. We buried the cat in front of my cabin. Several of the residents wrote poems about it and read them at the funeral. They sang "for she was a jolly good yellow" (it was an orange-yellow female cat), and the director gave a speech and read from a typewritten commendation that said the cat had died in the line of duty. The director's name was Brodt also. I did not type much at Potopotawoc, and I did not read much either, except magazines, as I must have mentioned already. There were always fresh magazines in the Shed. And I had other animals too, raccoons and skunks that would come up onto the steps and even into the cabin if I left the door open, and I would hear them scratching about at night. People said there were wolves, but I didn't believe them. I am not afraid of animals, if they are animals, though on one occasion it was a man who had become lost from the Shed. Once some-one invited me to play in one of their ball games, and when I refused he handed me the ball anyway, shoved it into my hand, but when the play started I didn't know what to do with the ball and just stood there until someone pushed me down in the mud. Living in Mexico, during the period when we still thought of ourselves as peripatetic—packing up and moving at the drop of a hat, which a lot of people found amazing, and even referring to ourselves as gypsies—it was normal to look out a window at night and see a rat or two. Our house stood on a very narrow street, practically an alley, that became very dark at night, with only a single metal-shaded streetlight every block or two. The light on our block dangled from a cable stretched between our house and the one across the street, and it swayed in the slightest breeze, causing giant shadows to race up and down the façades of the houses. Neither of us slept at all well in Mexico, because of the heat and because of the radios in the other houses, and sometimes one or both of us would get up and go sit by the window, where it was slightly cooler on the nights there was a breeze. Our bedroom was on the second floor and sitting at the window we could see rats creeping on the broken pavement beneath the streetlight; one could not sit there for very long without seeing them. Oddly, we scarcely ever saw one in the daytime, though they had to be hiding just everywhere. Clarence liked to say that rats were going to inherit the world some day—he enjoyed coming out with frightening generalizations of that sort. He carried lots of statistics in his head, most of them distressing, and he could go on a long time about them once he got started. He knew, for example, how many tons of rice are eaten every year by rats in Indonesia. He recited the figure one night while we were sitting at the window watching the rats, though of course I can't remember now how many tons it was, but it must have been a great many, or else why would he have told me? A fabulous memory for statistics was one of his annoying traits, though it impressed some people— impressed some men, I ought to say, since I don't suppose many women were impressed by it. I was never able to understand how someone could want to be an artist and also want to know a lot of statistics, though I never said that to Clarence in so many words. His statistical streak made it practically impossible for anyone to win against him in an argument, since just when you had him cornered he would trot out some figure or other, rattle it off the top of his head, that would show how wrong you were. I was never sure he had not made those statistics up for the occasion. He was capable of doing that, of making things up in order to win, a function, I suppose, of his ruthless side. Compromising principle when it came into conflict with getting ahead and not even batting an eye was the way he was ruthless in general, and inventing things was the smallest part of it. I am not making headway. And pages falling on the floor is the least of it. I am struggling to forge ahead, a few days ago I was in fact forging ahead, and here I am bogged down again, in the rats in Mexico. I don't care about the rats in Mexico.

Potts has fallen from a horse and fractured something, her tibia, I believe he said, the person who called, and a wrist, he being a relative of some sort, though he had what I thought was a thick German accent, and will not return before the end of summer. That might be for the best, though it means putting up with her rat for a while longer. Lately I have scarcely noticed Nigel, except to feed him and slap his tank when he thumps or whirs excessively. I enjoy having the building to myself. It is the first time this has happened for a lengthy period. Potts underneath me now, at this stage, would be disruptive and annoying, not the noise she makes, because she scarcely makes any, but the vapors of her mute presence filtering up through the floor, her silent existence seeping into my life. Imagine going up to someone in the grocery store and saying words like those—they would think I am crazy. If it happened to me, if I were that other person, would I consider it a sign of being crazy? Probably. How bizarre to think of Potts on a horse.

I was working a crossword a few minutes ago when I noticed the bite marks on my new pencil, four wedge-shaped indentations up near the eraser. I had not noticed them until I turned the pencil end to end in order to rub out an entry and in so doing transferred my grip to the upper (now lower) portion of the shaft, where I felt the marks. I am not sure how long I have had this pencil. They have built a new elementary school just a few blocks from here, replacing the boarded-up one that I see from the kitchen window, and the children rushing to class, book bags jouncing on their backs, regularly shed pencils. Practically every week it seems to me I come across two or three lying on the sidewalk, and sometimes I pick one up, because I am feeling in need of a pencil, if I am planning to work a crossword, or because the pencil seems brand new, as this one did until I upended it. In the latter case (seeming brand new) I find these abandoned pencils irresistible, and I nearly always pick up such a one unless I am hurrying to get out of a rainstorm, and then I sometimes go back and fetch it afterwards, though I have not been doing that lately, because of the difficulty bending. The indentations on this pencil, therefore, were probably made by the teeth of a child, and in point of fact they are quite small, smaller than the ones I have just made with my own teeth for comparison. I don't chew pencils myself, or rather I don't chew pencils anymore, but when I did, just now, bite the pencil I was using for the crossword, just to see, the memory of the taste of the yellow paint came rushing back. As a child I loved getting new pencils, because I could chew the paint off them—scrape it off, actually, not chew, using my front teeth like chisels, carefully scraping so as not to damage the wood underneath, until no fleck of paint remained except for a very thin yellow line under the brassy metal band that holds the eraser and that you didn't want to touch with your teeth, because of the unpleasant electric sensation. To scrape away that last bit I would use the point of a thumbtack or, later, when we studied geometry, the sharp tip of my compass. I have pulled the fern away from the wall and with scissors cut off the parts that have turned yellow. There is now a rather large gap on one side, though it is greener overall. It is smaller but greener. I could trim the other side, to even it up, the way Papa used to do the hedges. I won't try to carve an animal, though. I tore the note about the library books off the window but have not been able to get the remnants of tape off, even after scraping with a kitchen knife. I don't have a razor blade, which is what the window washers used. I imagine the glue has hardened with age. How old is it, I wonder. Some of the notes have turned yellow and brittle, especially the ones I wrote on scraps I tore out of magazines. Some are in marker, either black or red, while others are in ballpoint or pencil. Those in pencil would be ones that came to me while I was working a crossword, probably, as I don't use a pencil otherwise. One on a yellowed index card says Write Lily. It has been a great many years since I thought of writing Lily. In order to reach a place where I could stand and scrape the window I had to walk on my pages, and twice there was a crunching sound when I stepped. It was not snails, of course, though that was my first thought also. Some of the glass from the shattered picture frames must have shot underneath. Clarence loved pistachios and was constantly dropping the shells on the floor to be stepped on. I suggested he put them in his pocket, if it was too much trouble to throw them in the trash can. He said he was not going to walk around town with a lot of shells in his pockets. Of course I was not suggesting that— I thought he could empty them in the garbage can in the kitchen before he went out. And it was scarcely a town at that point—the place we had ended up in at that point was scarcely a town, just a diner, a filling station, and a lot of shut-up houses in three rows on a strip of sand between a marsh and the ocean. He ate a lot of pistachios there while he worked, so as not to drink. I bring up the pistachios now, even as I try to forge ahead, because when I crunched the glass I got a pang. And now there are footprints on my pages, entailing more pangs. I could, I suppose, make this into nothing but a list of pangs and the items that cause them. That would be too short for a book, of course, though it could be most of an introduction, in case the Grossman woman is still interested. I can write and ask, I suppose. If I carve an animal, it will have to be a small one, without too many protuberances. During one of our best times, when Clarence and I were both frantically writing—not frantically, really, smoothly and rapidly—when we were staying in the Berkshires, in a kind of glorified cabin that friends had lent us, the floor was absolutely covered with discarded pages. One afternoon Clarence came back from shopping in town, in a hurry, I suppose, I don't recall the reason, and was rushing with his habitual long strides across the living room, when he slipped on the paper, just like stepping on ice, and fell flat on his back, groceries sailing off in every direction. He looked like someone is a slapstick movie, legs and arms in four directions and groceries flying up and raining down just everywhere. He did not find it funny, of course. He flew into a fury and refused to respond when I asked if he was all right. He gathered up all my pages—there were dozens and dozens—without a word, just shoveled them up with his hands by the armload and threw them out the front door, where the wind carried them across the meadow and into the trees. I stood at the window of the bedroom and watched them blowing across the field and into the orchard on the other side of the road. It rained that night, and the next day, when I went out to look, there were soggy pages everywhere, even in the trees. They were still there when we left two weeks later. The people who had lent us the cabin, and who were outdoor friends of Clarence's, went up the following weekend, and they did not say anything about the pages, though they could not have failed to see them. I could carve a beaver.

I was not always bothered by Clarence's whistling while he typed. I am not sure when it began to bother me. I have a clear mental picture of him typing in our kitchen on Jane Street, standing at the counter tapping away and whistling, and I don't get the sense that I minded then. He always typed standing in the early days, and later, after we left Jane Street for Philadelphia, he designed a special stand for holding the typewriter at the perfect height and angle, constructing it himself in the studio of a sculptor he knew who lived in a barn in New Jersey. It was held together with wing nuts, so we were able to take it apart and carry it with us each time we moved. It was the only piece of furniture that we kept from one place to another, unless one considers things like tripods, guns, and typewriters to be furniture; I would classify those as equipment. Much later, when he had become the heavy rather bullish man of his middle years, he sat down to type. I think it fair to say that his writing sat down also. He would hand a piece to me and I would notice how leaden it was, and I would make suggestions and offer encouragement. "*Allegro*," I might say, as encouragement, "*allegro con brio*, Clarence," and I once suggested he cross out every other sentence. It was in a fit of pique that I suggested that, I think. After the first three or four moves, it dawned on me that we were never going to stay anywhere for long, and I fell into the habit of throwing away my typed pages. There were always boxes of them, I had no interest in them anymore, and they were constantly in the way. I suppose they were furniture rather than equipment, especially considering that when the boxes had become a stack we would often keep things on top of them; and since they were furniture, we left them behind when we moved. Clarence had a great deal of equipment, which he called gear, most of it having to do with hunting or fishing. I hunted and fished too but did not have equipment of my own; I used whatever

Clarence handed me. He would have liked to possess a house full of heads, plus spears and guns and so forth, all up on the walls, as in the hunting lodges he saw when he went on hunts with wealthy people, when he was reporting for magazines. We had just one head, of a huge deer he shot in Wisconsin and paid somebody to stuff. We lugged the head about with us for years, and one of the first things he would do on moving into a new place was nail it up. He liked to sit in a chair, stare up at the head, and talk to it. Unless he was drunk, he would be joking when he talked to it. He pretended the head was his factotum. If we were about to go out somewhere, he might look up at the head and say, "Porter, fetch my jacket." What he meant, of course, was for me to fetch his jacket. In Mexico something began to eat the head, and eventually it became so mangy and moth-eaten we dumped it out at the beach house. That was the year Clarence decided to become a pharmacist again. The only equipment I still have, if you don't count kitchen equipment, is this typewriter, unless you count the radio. Speaking of which, it is sixteen past nine, the radio has just announced, and in a few moments we will hear Bartok's *Concerto for Orchestra*. Sixteen past nine *p.m.*, that is.

Even in the fullness of his power, Clarence was not an imaginative writer. When he became wildly inventive it was usually in a dishonest way, such as the time he wrote a long article about a trip to South Africa that included shooting a rhino (which he later changed to a hippo) that was charging him and that fell dead inches from his toes. It turned out the

African guides had already shot the animal, several times, it was staggering out of the bush mortally wounded and didn't even know Clarence was standing there, probably, when he shot at it. He was with his friend Denis Zimmerman, who told everybody the real story. Or the fake interview he did with himself—conducted in the bush by a South African journalist, supposedly—and tried to sell to *Esquire*. They saw right through it, of course. When word got out and people asked him about it, he pretended he had meant it as a farce, trying to shift the blame to the magazine for not getting the joke. It was not a joke, though. When Clarence was correcting a typescript he tended to chew the erasers off his pencils. He didn't eat the erasers, just chewed them and spit the little pieces out on the floor or picked them off his tongue and flicked them there. The pencils were worse than useless after he had done that—useless, I mean, for crosswords or anything where you are not absolutely certain of something the instant you write it down, because once the eraser has been chewed off a pencil it is left with a sharp metal scraper on one end. Failing to notice that some pencil I had happened to pick up was one that Clarence had been gnawing on, I would set out to erase something and end up gouging a hole in my page. I erase vigorously, so it was sometimes a large hole, a gash or rent, actually. So I fell into the habit whenever I came across one of those pencils of immediately tossing it in the trash can, in that way insuring that I would not pick it up by accident later. If Clarence saw me doing that, he would call out, "Hey, that's a perfectly good pencil." He would say the same thing every time, shout it, actually, even though he knew how it irritated me to hear him begin a sentence with "hey." One instance in particular stands out. I had just thrown away the last pencil in the house, because he had eaten the eraser as usual. He had been going over the proofs of one of his stories, and he had to stop in order to dig through the garbage in the kitchen and fish out the eraserless stub he had been using, and he was cursing under his breath while he was doing it. When he found it finally, it was covered with tomato sauce, and he turned on me. Holding the pencil high above his head, as if he thought I might snatch it—it looked like a bloody dagger—he accused me of being envious because I did not have any proofs of my own to correct. I had no proofs to correct, it was true, but I was not envious; I just didn't want my pages gouged. I had not always been irritated when he began a sentence with "hey"; it once had a different ring. In the first weeks after we met, when we were together constantly and tramping all over the city, if he wanted to call my attention to something, he would say, "Hey, Edna," and I would turn back and look. In that remark, about me being envious, with its insinuation that correcting proofs is in some way a superior activity to typing, you have Clarence in a nutshell. That he was capable of coming out with an assertion like that, even provoked by someone who had just thrown away his pencil, shows how far he was from grasping the difference between us.

"At the threshold of art I stand dazzled and amazed"—that is how it was with me once, that was the only way I knew to get beyond the banality of everyday life, which was crushing me. Clarence, because of his background, I always thought, was simply unaware that art could do this; I don't think it ever happened to him, and like the rest of them he gradually became bored with literature. And now it has stopped happening to me. I can spend hours at the window, watching people on the sidewalk below, watching clouds even, spend them not happily but not sadly either; I open a book and fall instantly asleep. Now the rat's wheel has developed a squeak, a tiny *yeep* at the same point in each revolution. For a long time we had talked about moving to the country, where "country" was a negative concept: no bars, restaurants, boozy friends, or parties. Going to the country was like opening a new chapter. Clarence did not say he was opening a new chapter then, though, as he did later, when he said it in connection with Lily. He said instead, "I've got to turn this thing around," where by "thing" he meant his life. In the end we did not go to the country, we went to the beach instead, to a little down-at-the-heels resort he had visited once for three days with his family when he was nine years old. That was the first time most of them had left the mountains, and it was Clarence's first glimpse of the ocean. They could only afford a single room in a motel twenty miles inland from the beach, five of them sleeping in one room and three in the car. Clarence liked to tell this story, adorned with meticulous detail, to show people how impoverished he had been as a child. He would slip into a kind of reverie while he was telling it, staring into the distance as if reciting the events on a film he was watching, but when he had finished, instead of being saddened all a person could think was how happy Clarence had once been for three days when he was nine. The resort was not a rousing place even in summer, I imagine, and it had shut down for winter by the time we got there. We drove down the main street and unloaded our bags at a cottage at the end of it. An hour later Clarence was standing in a phone booth talking to one of his friends in New York, saying, "It's not a town, it's a shipwreck." The place was, I can say now, the perfect mirror of our mood, as if a deep psychic undertow and not just Clarence's childhood fantasy had drawn us there. In the slanting light of the winter sun the main street had a desolate evacuated look, when we drove down it the first day, long shadows asleep on the pavement and a fine gritty dust blowing across it. Most of the houses were shuttered, only a small restaurant and a filling station still open for business. The beach had been slowly washing away for decades, since before Clarence's childhood visit, probably, a strong lateral current steadily dragging the sand southward, and it was now just a narrow strip of sand as steeply sloping as a riverbank, whitened stumps of salt-killed cedars jutting from the sand here and there. At high tide the ocean came up under the houses closest to the beach, most of them abandoned, swirling around the pilings. Every year, people told us, one or two houses were swept away by big winter storms. None were swept away the winter we were there, though one burned down and another was demolished on purpose. From our windows we would watch them ripping it down. In an effort to stop the erosion of the sand a series of stone and wood jetties had been constructed perpendicular to the beach and jutting far out into the surf, so that walking down the beach one had to climb every few hundred feet over piles of rock and creosoted timber encrusted with weeds and tiny mussels. Most of the still-inhabited houses were run-down and dilapidated, their owners probably reluctant to sink money into structures tied so firmly to the whims of hurricanes. Our cottage was not big, but it was right up against the ocean: spring tides lapped at the base of the stairs, and the wind whistled in the screens. "It's a dump," Clarence judged at the end of our second day. I told him I liked it. It was white with blue shutters, I think, though I might be confusing it with a cottage in Falmouth that we rented for two weeks one summer. Every morning and afternoon, unless the tide was high and we could not walk on the beach at all, we took long, icy windswept promenades by the sea, clambering, as I mentioned, over jetties, and in between the walks Clarence sat in the house and tried to write and not take a drink until supper.

Rain last night, cooler this morning. I went out after the sky cleared, intending to walk over to the park, and on the way there almost fell down on the sidewalk. I didn't fall down entirely; I sat down suddenly when I became dizzy, on someone's front steps, in order not to fall down. This had happened before. My feet and fingers tingled, though, and that does not usually happen, and I thought, Well, this is a bad sign. I wondered if I ought to breathe into a bag. I didn't have a bag, not expecting something like this to happen when I set out, even though it had, as I mentioned, happened before without the tingling, so I suppose I ought to carry a bag just in case. I could carry a bag of bird food, which I ought to do anyway, and dump the food out on the sidewalk if it happened before I reached the park. Sparrows would take care of it, I am sure, even if none were present at that moment. I wonder if they smell food, like a dog, or do they recognize it by sight. A grain of millet, I think, would appear extremely small from up where they are. Perhaps they land on the sidewalk randomly, just to hop around, and then they see it. If it happened in a store they would not want me dumping bird seed on their floor. On the other hand, being a store, they would have plenty of bags, and they could just give me one. I have never personally breathed into a bag. I was thinking about it then only because I have heard that dizzy people need to do that, because they have too much oxygen. On the other hand, I thought, maybe I was dizzy from too little oxygen, which can also happen, I believe, in which case breathing into a bag would be a mistake. So I sat there, feeling helpless and agitated, until it passed, whatever it was, what people in the old days would have called a spell, probably. I could almost hear someone saying, "Edna is having another one of her spells," the implication being that I was just putting on. Nigel seems to be spending more time in his tube. I think he does not enjoy being constantly looked at. I hardly ever look at him, but he might not know that, my eyes from a distance probably appearing quite small to him. Or he is afraid that I will throw something at him. If I were Nigel I would not like living in a glass house like that. Never get away from Edna's eyes, the way Edna could never get away from Brodt's eye.

I wonder if he even knows that those things are my eyes. The glass-paneled building I worked in might just as well have been made of glass all the way through, a five-story aquarium. I am tempted to say that when Nigel sees me, sees my big eye peering at him through the glass, I remind him of Brodt, though of course that makes no sense at all. Clarence began work on a new novel. For the first three or four weeks, after he started, he would sometimes cut our walks short in order to rush back to the house, practically bounding over the jetties, scrambling actually, cursing the sharp barnacles and mussels, and I would hear the sound of the typewriter when I climbed the steps from the beach. He did not show it to me this time, but one day when he was out shopping for groceries I went into the room and read it, and I saw that it was not good. Each time I looked in the weeks that followed the increment of progress had grown smaller, and I could tell that he was giving up. Listening at the door I could hear him giving up, hear him moving about in the room, opening books and slamming them shut, opening and closing a window, getting up and sitting down, the chair creaking, a sigh, a rat-a-tat from the typewriter and a long silence, another rat-a-tat, and it was time for lunch. This was the epoch I mentioned earlier, when he ate pistachios so as not to drink and ended up having pistachios with his highballs. And that was when we threw out the deer head, pitched it into the surf, where it floated, only the muzzle and antlers out of the water, a terrible image of drowning, before flipping over and becoming just a plank bobbing on the waves. We stayed on until the weather was warm again. After Clarence had given up he passed a few weeks fishing practically from dawn to dusk, standing at the edge of the surf, holding the rod and looking out to sea, and once when I went out and stood beside him he pointed and said, "Over there is Africa." Of course he was not fishing in the sense of caring whether he caught anything—watching his future vanish, I imagine, hull down on the horizon, is what he was really doing. I can see him in my mind's eye, from above, as seen by someone standing on a high bluff, in an icy wind, and the words that come to mind are "bereaved" and "bullheaded." He cooked everything he caught—drum, flounder, whiting, ray, shark, toadfish, croaker, catfish, eel—and ate them with bitter gusto. I ate rice and tiny pale Le Sueur peas from a can, and we faced each other across the table in the neon-lit kitchen. I don't remember what we talked about. I had once said to him, soon after we first met, that it was the nature of artists to fail, that if they did not fail it was because they were not any good. But that did not help now, because he knew that their failure was not the sort of failure that was happening to him now. I moved my typewriter into the room he had vacated, because it looked out on the ocean and I could be at my station when the sun rose from the Atlantic, the same as today, except the ocean today is an ice cream factory. Clarence had been putting on weight for years; I gradually had grown accustomed to thinking of him as a heavyset person. His physical presence was dominating, chairs and floors creaking beneath him. One morning while we were out walking the wind snatched the straw hat I was wearing and sent it cartwheeling down the beach, and Clarence set off in pursuit, lumbering to catch it before it bounded into the waves. He reached it just in time and was walking back toward me, when he placed the hat on his head, as a joke, and I saw, suddenly, that he was positively fat. This was, coincidentally, the same day he announced out of the blue that he was becoming a pharmacist again. That was why I suddenly saw him fat, probably, because I was prepared to look at him differently. Meanwhile I was growing thinner, the flesh melting from my thighs and hips, my breasts vanishing. When we walked together on the beach I thought we were like Body and Spirit. Clarence was Body. I was Spirit.

Of course Poole might not have picked up his typewriter from the store at all; he might, in his distress, have forgotten he had left it there. How would I feel, if one day I decided to commit suicide and could not find my typewriter? Desperate, I suppose. I cannot imagine a situation in which I would forget where I had left my typewriter. The squeak is worse. I hear it even with my muffs on: *yeep*, whir, *yeep*, whir, *yeep*, whir.

I have taped the lion photograph back up on the window. If one bears in mind that it was taken in nineteen sixty-four, it says something else about Clarence, different from what I suggested earlier, when I observed how true to life it was, being a picture of him with a drink in his hand. In nineteen sixty-four Hemingway had been dead for years and nobody but Clarence was still shooting lions, and that, I think, was the tragedy of his life, that he was, in a sense, left to shoot lions alone, having made his appearance onstage at the moment they were closing the theater. I say tragedy, but it was also comedy: the lights have come up, the audience has left the building, women in kerchiefs are vacuuming the aisles, and someone is still up there on the stage. He is wearing laced boots and a cartridge vest and is earnestly performing a role that he learned in school, though with increasing weariness as time passes. He pauses now and then to nip from a flask. The tragedy was that his position in life had become comical, I mean, and he had failed to notice. *Shooting Lions Alone,* I think, would make a good title for a book. For a biography of Clarence, of course—it could not be the title of a book Clarence himself might have written, because he could not be ironic about himself, and he did not like it either when I became ironic about things that he took seriously. Oddly, the one thing I was never ironic about, which was my typing, he was ironic about, calling it "Edna's remembrance of everything past." Despite his consuming desire to be the next new thing, there was something old-fashioned about Clarence, even quaint—I say that, knowing how it would have piqued him. And to make matters worse, it is impossible to consider someone like Clarence quaint without being ironic. Perhaps *old-fashioned* is not the word—I mean conventional: the B-movies he worked on, and the outdoor stories that people said were wonderful when they appeared but rapidly forgot about, and the stuff he published in the little literary magazines. He was not always proud of being the sort of writer he had become, and now and then he would still send something off to places like

Esquire and the *New Yorker*, though he always got preprinted slips in return, as I had warned him was bound to happen. In my opinion, when they reissue *The Forest at Night* no one will even notice. Shooting lions alone: because after a while I was not, speaking metaphorically, able to shoot lions with him anymore, or I was not willing to. I was unable to be willing after a point is how it was, a psychological spring or some such thing having become broken. I used to say to Clarence, when he was expatiating on something, with statistics, or reporting conversations from one of his literary drinking parties, that we were witnessing the end of civilization, and of course I meant our civilization, the one that has a place for people like us, like me and like Clarence some of the time. After typing the previous sentence I happened to glance over at the tank: Nigel's eyes were bulging. If I were to write a children's story, I might begin, "When the rat saw what she had written, its eyes bulged with astonishment." Can one write a children's story if one doesn't care much for children? I suppose I could make it frightening, it being easier, probably, to frighten things one doesn't care much about.

Sunday morning, and I don't hear the Connector, though the windows are wide open, or I barely hear it if I strain, when I hear the compressors also, and birds as well, and the voices of people on the sidewalk. One of the birds, which must be a robin, I hear even over the keystrokes, it is so loud, or a wren, maybe. It is the first time I have heard a wren here, if it is a wren. People passing in the street below can hear me typing, I am sure, and that makes me think of Capote's remark about Kerouac's book: "That's not writing, it's typing." He would say the same about this, presumably, if he were still alive and had a chance to read it. I suppose he meant that Kerouac's writing went on and on aimlessly. As if there were some other way in which one possibly could go on and on. This morning I became dizzy again, carrying my coffee from the kitchen. It seems to have become a habit. "Chronic" is the medical word for that kind of habit. I grabbed on to the bookcase and in the process spilled most of the coffee. I sat in the armchair awhile and then made another cup, which I have now allowed to get cold, sitting here sorting through the items I intend to type today; sorting in my head, as I said earlier. It is instant coffee, which I became accustomed to drinking when I had to save time, when I was still going to work—I was chronically drinking it—and I would also brush my hair on the bus, because I was always running late no matter how early I got up; did I explain about that? When I was late Brodt would write on a scrap of paper and then fold the paper up and slip it in his shirt pocket. I have an urge to toss things overboard, superfluous things and things that strike me as burdens and things that are not sanitary, like books. I have already mentioned mold, probably, but in case I have not, that is what I am referring to, as making books unsanitary. Of course, there is a sense in which this actually is a children's story, being all about what happened to Clarence and me as a consequence, in part at least, of having been the sort of creatures we were as children, of the lives we lived before we became ourselves, when it was too late to do anything about it. I am going to lie down now.

The moment I turned the corner, I saw the store was not there anymore. A sign in the window read Ethel's Hair & Nails, and someone had cleaned the window glass. A girl with a silver ring through one eyebrow was standing with her back to me when I entered, behind a chair in which an older woman was seated, doing something to that woman's hair, cutting it perhaps, though I don't recall scissors. When I came in they both looked at me in the mirror. "Can I help you?" the girl asked, talking to my reflection. She did not turn her head, so I looked away from the girl standing behind the chair with her back to me and spoke to the one facing me in the mirror. I told her I was looking for the man who used to run a typewriter repair shop in that building. The reflection said it did not know anything about that. "Maybe Ethel knows," it said. But Ethel had left for the day. I asked if there was a number where I could reach her, and added, "It's a long trip for me, I'm not sure I can come again." The girl said, "I'm not authorized to share that number," and then, speaking to the customer in the mirror: "So that's what it was. I saw all them old typewriters and I thought this must have been like a pawnshop or something." I said, "Typewriters? Where?" The real one turned to face me. "Around back. They're gone now, though." At the side of the building was a small parking lot—puddles of water in the broken pavement, clouds in the puddles. I walked across it and around to the back. Nail-studded boards, broken sheetrock, empty paint cans, and other trash were piled against a wall. A bundled sheet of paint-splattered plastic spilled water on my shoes when I pulled on it. The sheetrock was sodden and pulpy and came apart in my hands, and my shoes and dress were soaked and filthy by the time I had shifted enough trash to get a good look at the typewriters underneath: a dozen or so lined up against the shop wall, quite ordinary machines for the most part, all of them badly rusted. Steadying myself against the wall I pushed on the keys of one with the toe of my shoe—they failed to budge. The IBM Selectric was not among them, but the antique Underwood I had noticed before, that had belonged to a person with a long name I couldn't remember then, was. I turned the tag over with my foot—it was Mary Poplavskaya. I knelt next to that one and slipped my hands underneath, took a deep breath, and clambered to my feet, staggering, and struck my shoulder hard against the wall. The typewriter wasn't heavy, as typewriters go, but it was heavy for me, considering. Essaying it on my hip and then on my shoulder, I found that hugging it to my abdomen was best, though it forced me to walk with a broad waddle. I had to stop and rest twice on the way to the bus, sitting on the curb, and the second time a woman came out of a shop to ask if I was all right. The bus was not crowded, and I placed the typewriter beside me on the seat. When I reached home I practically threw it on the kitchen table, heaved it up on top of the breakfast dishes and broke a plate with a rabbit on it. My hands, my dress, and the insides of my arms were brown with rust. When I showered, the rust-tinted water swirling around the drain at my feet reminded me of the murder scene in *Psycho*. There are no Poplavskayas in the phone book.

My shoulder is still painful. I am not going to type today. This was typed with my left hand, slowly.

Ravel, Prokofiev, and several others, I believe, wrote left-handed pieces for the pianist Paul Wittgenstein, who had lost his right arm in the war. That would be the First World War. He was the philosopher Ludwig Wittgenstein's brother. I don't know which battle he lost his arm in—on the Eastern Front, maybe. I don't know the names of any of the battles on the Eastern Front in that war, though I know the names of a few of them in the next war: Kursk, Smolensk, Stalingrad.

Another of our extravagances, after the Africa trip, and after Mexico, was a year in France, when we lived all winter in a gigantic house in an absolutely tiny village. I might have already said something about that house, which was so big we started out by writing in separate rooms. We each had two rooms, one for the morning sun and another for the evening sun. It was early autumn when we came. A few weeks later the weather turned icy cold. The house had no heating system at all, just fireplaces, and by late December we were spending most of our time huddled next to the fireplace in the kitchen, a long room with a vaulted ceiling and a little window at one end. It was like living in a cave. Clarence stopped typing and wrote in longhand, with mittens on, and every afternoon, unless it was pouring rain, we took long walks through the countryside. In my memory we did not see the sun again after winter set in, but that can't be true. When I recall our walks, there seems always to be fog or drizzle. The countryside was fantastically bleak once the leaves had fallen, a dull-brown planate expanse, nothing resembling a proper hill, the fields bare and brown after the harvest: acres of clumped and furrowed earth without a trace of vegetation, separated by narrow woodlands of scrub trees and thickets. We never walked in the fields except to cross them in order to reach the woodlands beyond. At the edge of the village, visible from the kitchen door, stood a white cement signpost bearing the name Château-Thierry followed by number of kilometers. I have forgotten how many kilometers exactly—forty or fifty, I think it was. Seeing the name Château-Thierry every day when we were living there made me think a lot about the war, because of the monument on the hill perhaps, where I saw the name for the first time when I was just learning to read and where I finally understood that it was a place where a large number of people had suffered and died in wretched circumstances. "It was ghastly," Clarence said, referring to that war. He had books of photographs of that war. More ghastly than the images of dead soldiers, blasted trees, and dead horses, were the stunned and staring faces of the living. We sometimes walked across a field to reach the woods on the other side. The mud was gluey and tenacious; it clung to our shoes, more with each step, until we were compelled to stop and scrape it off with a stick. I rested one hand on Clarence's shoulder to keep my balance while I scraped. When the mud dried on the boots of the soldiers it became as hard as plaster of Paris. Sitting on the floor of the trenches they chipped at it with the points of their bayonets. If they fell facedown in it when they were struck, the stretcher bearers, when they turned them on their backs, did not know who they were. Huge rats were everywhere in the trenches, feeding on the dead and the wounded. Clarence told me that rats crawled under the greatcoats of the dead soldiers and chewed tunnels through the frozen bodies, and when they lifted a corpse to bury it a dozen rats might tumble out. We did not have rats or mice in France, because the house came furnished with two cats—a gray female called Chatte Grise and a black male called Chat Dingue. Chat Dingue means Krazy Kat in French. The mud never dried the winter we were there, though sometimes it froze, and on the coldest days we were able to cross the fields without sinking. The whole time we lived in France that winter I thought about the suffering of the soldiers, which was so different from the way I suffered. I did not know how to compare it to my suffering. I did not know how to measure either of them.

There is an incongruity. Maybe events in the world are too big for words. War is too big. They, the words, are like tiny insects banging against a windowpane (the "window of the mind") trying to get out, and outside is the big tumultuous world. Or maybe it is the other way around: it is the words that are too big; some words are too big. The word "love" is too big. Maybe the word "Clarence" is too big as well. I used to think the mute, incoherent daily suffering of ordinary life was too big for words. Now I think the words are too big for it. There are no words trivial enough to say how terrible it is.

Yellow police tape surrounded the site, but people were lifting it and walking under. I walked right up to the edge of the hole: a rectangular cement-lined crater, twisted iron pipes projecting from the walls. Except for the pipes it could have been the roughing-in for a swimming pool. Concrete steps descended into the hole on one side, but I did not try to go down them. There were several other people there, standing about vaguely or taking pictures. There was nothing to see, just the hole with a great heap of debris at one end of it and a small bulldozer next to that. The bulldozer was not running. I didn't see anyone who looked like he belonged there. Some of the neighboring houses had plywood sheets blocking the windows, trash and debris littered sidewalks and lawns, and the street gutters were full of ashy mud. A tall man came and stood beside me. He said, speaking to no one in particular, "Not much to see, is there?" I made a small noise. I was turning to go, and he handed me a flyer: I was invited to visit the Tabernacle of Praise Church of God in Christ. If this city were bombed, there would be thousands of holes like that one. I have, despite myself, formed a picture of Henry Poole: standoffish, weird, late-night walker, a big man, probably, people remarking on the smallness of his dog. He was a prolific writer of something, I think, owning such a large, expensive typewriter; of letters, most likely. "Ungainly fifty-two-year-old lonely TV repairman" sums him up, I suppose, for the rest of us. A stooped, overweight man with a hanging lower lip, is how I picture him. He had lugged that heavy IBM Selectric typewriter all the way across town to be repaired, because he had something important to write, I imagine. Concealed in his character were aspects of the artist, revealed by this determination to finally set it all down on paper, to confide it there. The fact that his note was not going to survive the explosion would not have troubled him, the fate of what he wrote did not, I think, even interest him. If he ever spoke of his desire to set it down—to whom would he have spoken of it?—he would have used the phrase "get it all out," I think. He wanted, finally, to get it all out. He would not have thought of himself as an artist, though, and would not have been weighed down by the feelings of responsibility one gets when one thinks of oneself in that way. He would have been amazed to learn that I once wanted to be famous. Nigel won't stop squeaking his wheel, despite my shouts.

I sprang up so precipitously I knocked my chair over on its back. Trying to kick it out of the way, I managed to tangle a foot in the rungs and nearly fell. I caught myself by grabbing hold of the typewriter and almost dragged it off the table. A chain reaction begun by the rat, who pushed first— pushed psychologically, of course, not with his paws: the relentless squeak of his little wheel was pushing. "A final squeak knocked Edna from her chair" was how it felt, I suppose. I snatched a pencil from the table and stamped across the room. Nigel's eyes bulged when he saw me coming. I am sure he thought I was going to stab him with the pencil. I leaned over the tank, nose almost touching the wire screen. I shouted down into it as loud as I could and smacked the glass side with the flat of my hand, smacked it so hard that I am surprised I didn't break it. Nigel flew straight into the air. I thought for a second he was going to topple over backwards, but he caught himself in time and shot into his tube. I waited to make sure he was not going to rocket back out before lifting the wire top. After a minute with neither hide nor hair of him, I reached inside and jammed the pencil down through the spokes of his wheel. I must have really frightened him—it was a long time before he came back out. He climbed in his wheel and tried to make it spin, then he sat in it, scratching. I don't know why I said feelings of responsibility, when I meant feelings of failure.

A blank of days, days of blank. I did not type a word, I slept a great deal, I ate. I went down to Potts's place. Despite my sporadic efforts several of the plants are intent on dying. I sat in Mr. Potts's chair and watched the fish—subaqueous flowers afloat in a green fusion. From the window ledge a few feet from where I sat a plant had littered the carpet with yellow leaves. I dwelled, I thought, like Keats, among sere leaves and twigs. I fell asleep in the armchair and had a dream in which I was presenting a young Clarence to Papa, though in reality Papa died before I ever met Clarence. In the dream, instead of "Papa, this is Clarence," I said, "Papa, may I present Sir Nigel Poole," and Clarence bowed deeply, with a sweep of an ostrich-plumed hat. On other days I walked over to the park. Once I fell asleep on a bench there and dreamed of the gardener and the mole. After putting the mole in his pocket, he began jumping about, hopping from foot to foot, and then he stopped, unzipped his fly, and pulled out a rat. Nurse put her hands over my eyes and made me turn and run away. We paused in the driveway by the house, I looked up, and there was Papa seated on top of a hedge. Nigel has made bite marks up and down his pencil.

I did not hear the buzzer. I opened the door to take the trash out, and Brodt was standing on the landing—a different Brodt, I am tempted to say, owing to the elegant brown suit, collar noosed tight by a blue-and-yellow striped tie, and owing, I think, to the expression on his face. Well, he was smiling, and he was not wearing his uniform, and I did not for a brief moment know who he was, which is odd, as I had been expecting him since the day I glimpsed him staring up at my windows, if that was Brodt in fact and not, as I suggested then, someone who had come about the gutter. I was so agitated during his visit that I forgot to ask if it was him before. Perhaps not agitated, implying that I was thrashing about, however slightly—*disquieted* is how I was, the whole time he was here. I told him how surprised I was to see him, and he nodded slightly. I stood aside and he walked in. I left the bag of trash on the landing. He was wearing a brown hat with a narrow rim, not quite a bowler, that looked as if he had found it in a cinema—found it inside a movie, I mean, not on one of the seats; an older British movie that would have been. He carried a black satchel on a strap over his shoulder. He took the hat off—it must have been rather tight as it left a red line across his forehead—and smiled again, disclosing a gold tooth. I held out my hand, and he handed me the hat. I walked behind him, carrying the hat, while he circumambulated the room, stepping around my pages and pausing now and then to examine some object, because he was looking for something, as I thought at the time, or because he didn't know what to do with himself, as I think now. He picked up a little soapstone Buddha from the windowsill and turned it over in his hand, looking, I assumed, for an identifying mark or label on the bottom, and placed it back. He paused by the sofa and stared down at the heap of books and photographs I had pushed off onto the floor, nudging some of it aside with the toe of his shoe, in a manner I thought inquisitive, though he might have been, in a very tentative way, clearing a space to sit down. If the latter was the case, he thought better of it, for he went over and stood at one of the windows plastered with notes, reading them perhaps (his back was to me), or else peering out between them at the ice cream factory, and I heard it roaring for the first time in a while, heard it, I want to say, with his ears. When he turned back to the room, he seemed to veer in the direction of the typewriter, which still held a page I had been typing, and he seemed to bend slightly, and I thought for a moment he was going to lean over the machine and read it. Pointing to the armchair, I suggested he take a seat, and he did, sliding the satchel from his shoulder and setting it on the floor in front of him. I sat on the edge of the sofa, facing him, the hat resting awkwardly on my knees. I considered placing it on the floor but did not want to appear to be discarding it. He looked down at the pages scattered on the floor next to chair. He glanced up at Nigel, who was peering at us through the glass. He made a series of little squeaking sounds in Nigel's direction, lifting his upper lip and sucking through his teeth—the rat did not give any sign of hearing. "Would you like coffee?" I asked. He did not want coffee. He would enjoy a glass of water. I placed the hat on my seat and went to the kitchen. When I returned the hat was on the floor beside the chair. I handed him the glass and sat down again. He took a sip of water and placed the glass carefully on the floor next to the hat. I noticed he was looking at my pages again. He cleared his throat and leaned forward with a little smile that I did not know how to interpret, not being able to tell if it was sly or shy. I thought, Now he is going to talk about seeing me taking things. He bent down and snapped the satchel open. "I have something for you," he said. He reached into the satchel. A moment's pause, and he extracted my sheepskin earmuffs. "My favorite muffs," I exclaimed in a whisper, snatching them from him. I put them on. The world went suddenly soft. I took them off (the world rushing back) and held them on my knees. I am sure I was beaming. He placed both hands on the chair arms, elbows crooked, as if about to stand up. He looked intently at me and said, "I had an uncle who heard voices, had heard them ever since he was a child. At some point, after he was already grown and had a wife and children, if you can believe it, he discovered that if he wore earmuffs he wouldn't hear them anymore, hear the voices anymore." I started to speak: "I don't hear . . ." But he continued, "In the summer it was too hot for earmuffs, so he went around with big wads of cotton sticking out of his ears. A tall, really scrawny guy with a long nose, he looked just like a bird, some kind of crane, with downy tufts on the sides of his head. He looked really comical. Funny thing is, his name was Robin Bird." He chuckled slightly. I think I did not smile, I was so taken aback. I was expecting him to talk about staplers. He must have noticed my puzzled look. He dropped his eyes, looking down at my pages again. "I feed birds in a park near here," I said brightly, intervening, "sparrows and pigeons." And he said, "In a tree outside my window I have seen blue jays, crows, orioles." "I see only sparrows and pigeons," I replied. He went on, "They trumpet outside my window in the morning. On Sunday morning they wake me up when I'm trying to sleep." "Pigeons and sparrows wake me too, when they accumulate on the fire escape," I said, helping, "though of course they can't trumpet." "Whistling and trumpeting. Mostly whistling," he said. "That might be a cardinal," I said, "Cardinals whistle." He looked directly at me: "Yes, a cardinal. And something else too, in the top of a tree." He was silent a moment. Then, pointing to the muffs in my hand, he said, "Nice color." "Yes" I said, "I like blue," and added, "I don't have any trees, so I only get sidewalk birds like pigeons and sparrows." "Orioles and cardinals are the only colorful ones I see," he said. "Compared to sparrows," I observed, "blue jays are colorful." He laughed. "When I was a boy we hung aluminum pie pans on strings to keep birds out of the garden, but the blue jays weren't frightened." "I used to throw breadcrumbs out my window for the sparrows," I said.

"That's nice," he said. "We didn't have a feeder, because we didn't want to attract birds to the garden." There was a long pause. He shifted in his seat, leaned an elbow on the chair arm and then seemed to think better of it and placed one hand in the other, resting both in his lap. I said, "Would you care to look at some of my pages?" He stared at the papers on the floor again. He seemed to be considering. "No, I don't think that would help," I think he said, finally. "I mean, I prefer not." We seem to have said other things, which I have forgotten. We were standing in the doorway, he was turning to leave, when I said, "I was afraid you had come about the things I took." I hesitated. "All the things I stole from work." He made a sweeping gesture, as if casting something to the wind. "*Those* things?" For a moment I thought he was going to touch me on the shoulder, but he let his arm drop. "Don't worry," he said. "Everybody was taking things. Even the director was taking things." I closed the door behind him. I leaned against it. I heard his footfalls descending the stairs, and then, faintly, the street door open and close. I went and sat in my typing chair. It is dark now, night fell while I was typing, and I can't see the words. Oh, Brodt!

Nigel has eaten his pencil, all but the part inside the wheel and the metal bit that held the eraser, and he ate the eraser too, I noticed when I went over to give him a piece of my apple this morning—not eaten the pencil, actually, so much as shredded it; bits of blond wood and yellow paint are scattered about in the shavings.

After supper on the day following Brodt's visit, it was still light out, and I was at the window looking down on the people clustered at the bus stop across the street, when suddenly a small child, a boy, I think, broke from the crowd and ran into the street, directly into the path of a car. There was a tremendous screeching of brakes that for a moment I thought was the child screaming, and the car stopped. The rear of the car rose into the air as it was stopping, and then, after it had stopped, seemed to remain that way, tilted forward, as if aghast. Then the rear of the car settled slowly back, descending with a sighing sound, I thought. The little boy stood just a foot or so in front of the car's grill. From up here he seemed to be staring into the windshield. A woman in a blue dress rushed out of the crowd, wrapped the child in her arms and carried him back to the sidewalk. The two of them went a little ways off from the crowd. She knelt in front of the child, holding him at arms-length from her. I don't know how much time had passed, a few seconds or several minutes, when the car that had nearly struck the child began slowly to roll forward again, and that must have been the cue: as soon as it was rolling forward everything else started to move, the voices of the people at the bus stop floated up, I heard someone shouting, the child wailed, and all was just as before. I did not give Nigel any pellets this morning, as he has not touched the ones he has, that I gave him three or four days ago, when I fed him a big handful, or the apple, so he can't be hungry. I don't know how much a rat is supposed to eat, but this one is eating very little.

They forgot me at Potopotawoc. I was supposed to be there for just three weeks in the fall, officially there, as opposed to still there but forgotten, and they lost sight of me, despite the fact that I was right there in front of them day after day for almost two years; lost sight of me, so to speak, among the falling leaves; a year and eleven months. I say they forgot me, but of course that is a psychological remark, and I obviously can't know what was going on in their heads. Perhaps I was not forgotten at all, perhaps I was pointedly ignored. For two years I was ignored or forgotten. Given the silent treatment, sent to Coventry. Not entirely: sometimes I was paid too much attention, so they could not have forgotten that I was there, nor had Clarence, who sent postcards from all sorts of places, New Orleans, Key West, Tampa. They always ended, "and Lily sends her love." When I say that it is a psychological remark, I am referring to my own psychology. "For two years Edna lived abandoned and forgotten" was how it felt. One night a large group of campers came and built a bonfire in front of my house. I was afraid it was a lynching party. They stood around the fire laughing and talking and sometimes singing. Then they gathered in front of my door, and I opened it and stood in the doorway while they sang "It's a Long Way to Tipperary." Some of them spent the night there, sleeping on the pine needles beneath the trees. When the sun rose they wandered off, wrapped in their sleeping bags and blankets; in the dawn mist they looked like wandering monks. Several of them were like that, wrapped in robes, moving about in the fog under the trees, when time stopped, just as it stopped for the car and the little boy, briefly, and they became a painting. A moment later they were walking away again, grumbling and cursing. They left behind a great deal of litter, and the next day I went out and cleaned everything up, beer cans and bottles and paper wrappers and sticks tipped with bits of marshmallow, and I put it all in a plastic bag and carried the bag up to the Shed. I want to say that I emptied the bag on the floor of the cafeteria, but in fact I just thought of doing that, because of the mess they had left in front of my cabin. I could not think of anything to type at Potopotawoc. Sometimes I copied things out of magazines, I typed an entire issue of the *New Yorker*, including the ads. I might have done that more than once. Everything I typed there was meaningless. It has been a long time since I have dwelled on Potopotawoc, dwelled in the sense of turning it over in my mind and trying to understand, which is quite different from obsessing. I told Clarence I was not obsessing, that I was merely thinking about it. Sometimes I cried about it, sitting on a rusted combine or threshing machine or whatever it was, at the edge of the pine woods. Nigel can scarcely haul himself forward. His breathing seems to be more rapid, and it makes a clicking sound. I had not noticed his sides heaving like that before. He was this way when I awoke yesterday morning. I have moved his water bottle, attaching it so the spout is closer to his head. I sat at the kitchen table and cleaned and oiled Poplavskaya's typewriter. I tried to make it type and discovered the way in which it is broken: the carriage return mechanism doesn't work, a pawl that is supposed to engage the gear has snapped, so even though the keys all function, the typewriter is practically useless except for typing things that are one line long. I typed a postcard to Potts:

"Nigel is having the time of his life." I have not thought of anything else short enough to type. Very little in life is that short. The postcard came out smudged with oil and rust. It looks like a postcard written fifty years ago, as in a sense it is. And the business with the exploding house: I look back and think, Who was that woman? As if I had temporarily lost my way, lost my bearings and wandered off the road, so to speak, into a thicket, or had gone temporarily out of my mind. That would explain a lot. Out of my mind for a couple of weeks in certain respects, not out of it entirely or always. "Edna had a bee in her bonnet" is how my mother might have put it. And when I would refuse to stop typing, after he had been calling me for a while, Clarence would come to the bottom of the stairs and shout, "Are you out of your mind, Edna?" It was not a question. He might be sick, I suppose. He drags himself along in what could be construed as a sickly fashion, though that might be the way a rat of his age is supposed to walk for all I know, or the way a rat is supposed to walk on shavings. I did not pay attention to how he was walking before; maybe they all walk like that. How would I walk in wood shavings up to my knees? If he is sick it is from eating paint, probably. It might not be a book, it might be an introduction, or maybe a long preface.

I have posted a new note, taped it up next to the one that says: Feed the Rat. It makes sly reference to my interest in Henry Poole and his house, which seems strange to me now. I think I should call it my *erstwhile* interest, and that—my erstwhile interest—seems bizarre now, since I no longer know what there was about it that interested me. I am not making myself clear. It is like thinking that you have caught a fly, but then when you open your fist slowly, you discover there is nothing in it. You were holding your fist tightly shut, convinced you had a fly inside, and the whole time there was nothing in it, and it feels strange and bizarre and a little shocking when you open your fist and discover that. The new note says: "People in glass houses should not read newspapers." As a thought, this strikes me as puzzling and profound. Clarence said once that I never considered anything profound unless it was puzzling. He made that remark after I had told him *The Misfits* was not profound.

Someone was pushing the door buzzer. Or better: someone was buzzing at the door, that sounding more the way it felt from inside, from inside the apartment, I mean, the doorbell buzzing, the dour buzzer bellowing, and there was a buzzing of voices without. Now they are knocking. My thought is not to answer. I am not going to answer. It is Giamatti, I am sure.

I went to the window to see if I could catch a glimpse of whoever it was as they were leaving. I did not see anyone. I can't see the portion of the sidewalk that is right next to the building unless I lean far out, and I am reluctant to do that. Perhaps they didn't leave. I suppose it might have been Potts. If it was Potts and she went into her place after knocking, I would have heard the door opening and closing. I don't normally hear Potts when she is moving around inside her apartment, but I always hear her going in and out.

Anyway, it is too soon for Potts. I am going to have to change a lot of this, and I will want to leave Potts out.

I was standing at the window looking down, when I felt that Nigel had died. "Edna was invaded by an impression of sudden death behind her" was how it was. I turned around to see. He was inside the plastic tube with, as always, a portion of his tail protruding. I tapped on the glass but he did not stir, the tail did not twitch. I reached in and lifted one end of the tube; his head slid out the other end. His eyes were shut, mouth agape, incisors manifest. I lifted the tube higher in order to peek inside, and he slid most of the way out, dangling from the end of it. I dumped him directly from the tube into a Ziploc. Under the impact of his weight the bag slipped from my grip and struck the floor with a thump, a dull thud, I want to say, as of a dead thing, and he fell out. Using the tube and the edge of a foot I worked him back inside. He is in the freezer now, in the door to the freezer, as I don't want him on top of the vegetables.

At the agency yesterday, filling out more forms, running into more problems. They asked, "Where do you live?" And I said, "In hell." And the girl asked, "Where's that, ma'am?" I tapped my chest and said, "In *here*, in *here*." Ditto for occupation: they always have a blank for that one. I used to write "none" but discovered this suggests to them that I am unemployed, which is so far from the truth it is laughable. I tried to get around it by writing "waiter" instead, but that did not work either: they wanted the name of my employer, and when I said, "self-employed," they were incredulous. They had thought I meant a waiter on tables. They wanted someone to accompany me home, but I said no. I wanted to say to them, "When I had nothing . . ." I could picture myself with nothing, but the fact is I have always had a little bit. I have never had the courage to have nothing, to be nothing.

If lives had chapters, the final chapter in Clarence's life would open in a house with yellow-flowered wallpaper and close outside a sawmill in Georgia. We had driven south, almost to the Gulf, a rented trailer hitched to a our station wagon carrying everything we owned swaying wildly behind us. At one point during the trip, Clarence compared going down there, which is where he came from, though not that particular region of it, to an animal going to ground, a thing one normally says about hunted animals, when they go into a hole to hide. We unloaded at a small farmhouse with asbestos siding, yellow wallpaper, and a front porch that had collapsed on one side, belonging to the owner of the pharmacy where Clarence had found a job. Surrounded by pine woods, where there had once been fields, it was not a farmhouse anymore. There were no farmhouses anymore anywhere around, because the soil was exhausted, Clarence said; just widely scattered, insubstantial, and generally run-down dwellings inhabited by people who drove long distances to work every day. The pine woods were hot and dusty. The trees were not tall and they grew close together, stunted big-leafed oaks and gums mixed in with the pines. The woods smelled of dust and resin, and at night the insects were deafening. Abandoned farm machinery—I am not sure what kind of machinery, incomprehensible shafts, wheels, and teeth—lay scattered at the edge of the woods, vine-wrapped and rusted, with small trees growing up through the interstices. Every weekday morning Clarence put on a white coat and drove twenty-three miles to work at a drugstore in town, where he made the acquaintance of Lily, who worked at the drugstore also and dressed in blue, because she was not a pharmacist. The wallpaper was pale yellow with deep-yellow flowers, the same in every room. When we moved in it was hanging off the walls in places, and Clarence pulled on the loose pieces, kept pulling until they broke and left tapering torn streaks down the walls. He lived in that house for several years, with me at first and then with Lily, and then, when I came back from Potopotawoc, with me and Lily. He stopped being a writer there and died between the house and the town, when he ran off the road and hit a truck in the parking lot of a sawmill. When just the two of us lived there, he was still calling himself a writer and would show people his book and the magazines with his stories, but I don't think he really believed that he would become one again. I don't remember typing there. I have wondered sometimes whether he went on calling himself a writer after I left, or was he doing it only for my benefit, still. He probably did, though, since there was no one around who could know it was not true. I am not sure if Clarence died in the car or in the hospital. I am certain that at some point he was dead in the hospital. I might call it *The Book of Suffering*. I am referring now to Clarence's suffering. If he

could read this, he would say "Are you trying to be funny?"
He would mean, of course, am I trying to be ironic.

I let Lily sit in front the first time we all three rode in the car,
because she was the guest, though later, when she was denizen
and I interloper, it became customary for me to sit in back. I
chose to sit in back, I think, because I did not like Lily's head
appearing over the seatback next to me, when she leaned over
to talk to Clarence while he drove. She talked to him almost
constantly when we were driving places. Riding in back I
sometimes listened to them talking to each other, but usually
I looked out the open window at the exhausted soil, their
voices drowned by the wind, or I stretched out on the seat
bench and slept. Because the yellow-papered house was in the
middle of what Clarence called the dullest place in America,
they fell into the habit of taking road trips out of there, and
sometimes I went with them and sometimes I stayed behind.
Montgomery, Chattanooga, and Savannah are some of the
places they went without me, as I recall. They would send me
a picture postcard and be back before it arrived. Clarence
would bring the mail in from the box on the highway and say,
"Well, what do you know, Edna has a card from Savannah,"
if that was where they had been. Once when I went with them
we drove down to the Gulf and went swimming in the ocean,
if the Gulf of Mexico is an ocean. A gulf is part of an ocean,
of course, though it would be bizarre if I said we went swimming in part of the ocean, as if anyone could swim in a *whole*
ocean. On the way back we stopped for gas somewhere north
of Panama City. Across the highway from the filling station

was a sort of backyard theme park called Jungle Adventures or some such thing, and Clarence insisted on walking over there. He was fascinated by things like that, tawdry, run-down things, because of his childhood, which was full of them, heartbreaking things that he was not able to forget about. We bought tickets from a teenage boy sitting on the tailgate of a pickup truck parked at the entrance. Clarence later said the boy reminded him of himself when he was that age, though I failed to see the resemblance. The theme park consisted mainly of half-a-dozen life-sized African animals, several dinosaurs, and some picnic tables scattered about under the trees. The animals were made of a smooth hard material, plastic or fiberglass, I suppose, that rang hollow when you knocked on their sides. At the edge of the park, practically on the shoulder of the highway, mounted on a large plywood sheet supported at the back by a series of slanting two-by-fours, was a life-sized painting of a big-game hunter, quaintly Edwardian in khaki plus fours, high socks, and pith helmet. He was clasping an enormous, still-smoking gun, which Clarence thought was a .416 Rigby, and resting a foot on the head of a lion with a lolling purple tongue. There was an oval hole in the plywood where the hunter's face would normally be and that made the whole thing look like a painting by Magritte. The idea was to stand behind the plywood sheet and stick one's head into the hole and be photographed. First Lily and then Clarence put their head through while I snapped pictures of them. At this moment I can look up and see the photograph of Clarence that I taped to my window, in which he has a foot on an actual lion. I don't have the picture I took of him with his head in the cutout and a foot on a fake lion, but if I did I would tape it up next to the other. That would be ironic.

Potopotawoc was mostly a time without typing, except for copying, and later, when I came back from there to the house with flowered paper, that was nearly a time without typing. With Clarence gone all day in the car and the woods too hot and dusty to be pleasant to walk in, one might assume that I would have typed a great deal there, before going off, but I don't recall typing anything then either. I must have typed some, though: had I not typed at all during the summer we moved to the wallpaper house, I would remember it as a dry period. I don't remember it as a dry period. In the place where I live now, as I must have stated at the outset, I went several years without typing a word, when the typewriter sat in the closet, and those years are marked in my mind by the absence of typing, and I do think of them as the dry years. When I came back from Potopotawoc, though, I am sure I did not type. I stayed in the flower-papered house with Clarence and Lily. I stayed in bed a lot of the time, though I was not ill. I listened to them in the yard shooting cans with pistols, competing. It was winter and the house was cold. On sunny days I took long walks along the shoulder of the highway, because I did not like walking in the woods, which had been fields so recently they were more like thickets of small pine trees than a proper forest. I came back from Potopotawoc at the end of one summer, and I left again at the end of the following winter. Clarence and Lily stayed on; they remained with each other, as we agreed they ought, and I went away.

I can see myself in the past, as if I were standing outside my life, an observer with a camera. I can see myself, for example, with a group of friends running down the steps of Founders Hall at Wellesley or sitting across from Clarence in the dining room of the Norfolk Hotel in Nairobi. I can see from my expression that I was happy at those moments, I have no doubt that I was happy, but I am unable to *refeel* the happiness. The fact is, I cannot imagine it.

I am going to buy a red pencil. Red pencils never have erasers. They are for people who are certain.

I have not typed anything for days and days. Days and nights, I should say, because I sat at the typing table sometimes late into the night without typing. Something must be wrong with the compressors; they have grown suddenly louder, while I can scarcely hear the traffic in the street below. I am not sure that I want to type anymore.

A little while ago I was standing at the window when fire engines passed, and I did not hear the sirens, even without my earmuffs. Why am I saying this, when what I mean is, I did not hear them *loudly?* Because my thoughts are roaring, probably—roaring, I want to say, as loud as compressors on the roof of an ice cream factory. They are screaming, actually. "Edna's thoughts are screaming like moths." I don't know what they are screaming about.

Ineluctable undeflectable leeway. Hopeless helpless drift to the side, of a woman talking, talking, because there is nothing else left. I could ask why. Of course somewhere on some plane of existence there is always nothing left. Most people do not reside there, though. The question is, how did she get there? And why does she stay there? She puts food in her mouth, gets dressed, breathes. Is the world slipping from her? Is it getting small as if seen through a long tube? Is it becoming dark?

Report on her current condition: reflective, freighted with souvenir, lachrymose.

I have spent the last penny of what I had to live on this month. On a pastry and a latte at Starbucks.

"Not another word," I tell myself. No more typing. And no scribbling either, or smearing, or jotting. From now on silence. This is the last you will hear from me. o.k. Good-bye.

I think the fern is quite thoroughly dead. If I were old-fashioned British, like the hunter on the cutout, I could say it was beastly dead, which would be amusing, said of a plant.

Roaring. And above the roaring, knocking. Of course I am not off my rocker—*that*, one could say, is the whole problem.

The point is to keep on talking, where by "talking" I mean typing.

It is not even solitude, it is worse than solitude, it is a mind full of items.

All my life my bonnet was full of bees.

Knocking again, accompanied now by several voices, a woman's, not Potts's, louder, saying "Edna, I want to talk to you." They can hear me typing. It seems pointless to pretend I am not here. I am going to pause now. I suspect the next blank space will be the biggest. I am going to pause, answer the door (they are still there), but first I am going to wind a clean sheet on the platen. If this ever becomes a book, that will be the last page. Perhaps before I open, or after I open, with the help of whoever is out there, I will gather up all my pages from the floor. They will make a respectable pile, I think. Clarence would say, "That's quite a stack, old girl," probably. And then when I come back I will bring a red pencil. I will carry the stack over to the brown chair, and I will take some things out and put a lot of other things in, I suppose, and then I will see.

COLOPHON

Glass was designed at Coffee House Press, in the historic
Grain Belt Brewery's Bottling House near downtown Minneapolis.
The text is set in Fournier.

FUNDER ACKNOWLEDGMENT

Coffee House Press is an independent nonprofit literary publisher. Our books
are made possible through the generous support of grants and gifts from many
foundations, corporate giving programs, state and federal support, and
through donations from individuals who believe in the transformational
power of literature. Coffee House Press receives major operating support
from the Bush Foundation, the McKnight Foundation, from Target, and from
the Minnesota State Arts Board, through an appropriation from the Minnesota
State Legislature and from the National Endowment for the Arts. Coffee
House also receives support from: three anonymous donors; Elmer L. and
Eleanor J. Andersen Foundation; Around Town Literary Media Guides;
Patricia Beithon; Bill Berkson; the James L. and Nancy J. Bildner Foundation;
the E. Thomas Binger and Rebecca Rand Fund of The Minneapolis
Foundation; the Patrick and Aimee Butler Family Foundation; the Buuck
Family Foundation; Ruth and Bruce Dayton; Dorsey & Whitney, LLP;
Fredrikson & Byron, P.A.; Sally French; Jennifer Haugh; Anselm Hollo and
Jane Dalrymple-Hollo; Jeffrey Hom; Stephen and Isabel Keating; the Kenneth
Koch Literary Estate; the Lenfestey Family Foundation; Ethan J. Litman;
Mary McDermid; Sjur Midness and Briar Andresen; the Rehael Fund of the
Minneapolis Foundation; Deborah Reynolds; Schwegman, Lundberg &
Woessner, P.A.; John Sjoberg; David Smith; Mary Strand and Tom Fraser;
Jeffrey Sugerman; Patricia Tilton; the Archie D. & Bertha H. Walker
Foundation; Stu Wilson and Mel Barker; the Woessner Freeman Family
Foundation; and many other generous individual donors.

To you and our many readers across the country,
we send our thanks for your continuing support.

Good books are brewing at www.coffeehousepress.org